THE DEVIL AND MAX LARGENT

MICHAEL TOMLIN

a novel

THE DEVIL AND MAX LARGENT
Copyright © 2022 Michael Tomlin

All rights reserved. No part of this book may be reproduced or transmitted in any form or by any means, electronic storage, and retrieval system, except in the case of brief quotations embodied in critical articles or reviews, without permission in writing from the publisher. For permission, please contact: JMT Publishing, 838 Neopolitan Way #212, Naples, FL, 34103-3119; or email michaeltomlin@me.com

Published by
JMT Publishing
Naples, FL
www.MichaelTomlinAuthor.com
michaeltomlin@me.com

ISBN (paperback): 979-8-9850798-0-7
ISBN (ebook): 979-8-9850798-1-4
ISBN (audiobook): 979-8-9850798-2-1

Book design by Domini Dragoone, www.DominiDragoone.com
Images: © altanaka/123rf, Matt Barnard/pexels, Biletskiy Evgeniy/iStock
Author photo © Darren Miles Photography, www.darrenmiles.com

TO VIANDA

CONTENTS

Oh My God! 1
Three Things You Never Want to Hear 4
Leaving Without Grieving 13
You Humans Are Creating Hell on Earth 15
What Do You Say, Hemingway? 19
To Be in Hawaii 24
We Dropped the Charges 29
Billy Bob Baker, The Mover the Shaker 35
Is God a Woman? 42
The Oncologist 49
Why God Needs the Devil 55
The 'I Love Me Wall' 61
Demons 66
Buttercup 71
The Church of Latter-Day Whatever Happens Is Okay 75
What Is Hell Like? 80
Can Max Come Out and Play? 87
The World's Greatest Misconceptions 94
The Secret to All Religions 100
The Cold Mystery 106
The Worst Vice 110
Aloha Spirit 112
Listening to God 115
Worthy of God's Grace 121
Satan Get Thee Behind Me 122
On the Way to LA 125
Oh No, Not Here 128

Trading Places with Brad Pitt 130
Make Him Say It 132
Non-Stop to Hawaii, I Hope 134
Home.. 141
On The Queen's Highway...143
Our Essence 146
Miracle...147
Kohala by the Sea 149
Permanent Impermanence 152
What Have I Done? 154
Surrender..158
Going to Hospice 161
Night Brings the Light 169
Shock and Awe 171
God's Infinity Pool 180
It's Not You, Buckaroo..186
You Again..189
The Next Day..192
The Farmers Market 196
Find Someone Who Will Love You Forever 206
Revenge Is Overrated 218
Righteous 224
Back at the Ranch..228
The Artist 235
Dancing in the Rain 238
Michelle 245
Mauna Key Beach 254
I Am Ready 257

*You can't go back and make a new start,
but you can start right now and make a brand new ending.*

—James R. Sherman, PhD

1

OH MY GOD!

"Max. Max Largent! Wake Up. Wake Up. NOW!"

Startled, I jerk up in bed. "Who's there?" I shout, not knowing the source of my fear. I am sweating like a racehorse that just won the Kentucky Derby hauling a fat jockey. My head is covered in dampness, the pillow is soaked, and my tee-shirt is tangled and stuck to my body.

I must be dreaming. I want to be dreaming. Struggling to take in short quick breaths, I gulp and strain in a futile effort to be in control yet still fighting for air like a six-year-old trying to explain away his misdeed while every other word is a hiccup. I swivel my head left and right searching for the source of this strange voice and for a quick escape.

No presence to see or feel. Besides, if it is an immediate threat, then my best friend Rhett, an eight-year-old long-haired German Shepherd who nightly guards my bedroom door, would at least be howling or barking. Instead, he raises his big head, turns it down to the right, squints and looks at me like he's asking, "Are you crazy?" In this way-too-early-in-the-morning predicament, I am so much closer to crazy than okay.

Does this chilling deep dark voice want to do me in for some past transgression? If so, it will have to get in a long, long line.

Don't see or sense anyone, no shadow on the wall, no sheet with eye holes flying across my bedroom. Is God calling me home now? I thought I had more time. Wait a second. God doesn't have to give you a heads up or scare the 'BE-Jesus' out of you to call you home. Amazing how many nonsensical thoughts you can have in a nanosecond when terror is present.

"Quit asking so many questions and listen," the voice demands.

I fumble with the bedside lamp, desperate that light will frighten off whoever is there. Where are they hiding?

The room's stone cold when I throw off the covers. Funny, the last thing I do every night is turn the bedroom thermostat to 73 degrees. I wish this was funny.

Peeling off the damp clinging tee-shirt, I grab a robe from the bedside chair, throw it over my shivering shoulders, then bundle a wool blanket over myself like a kid building a fort. By feeling my face, I know the final verdict is in: Dammit. I am awake. All things considered, I would prefer being comatose.

Pleading in a sternly false bravado voice, I say, "What do you want? Who are you?"

"It's me, the Devil."

"Oh my God!"

"No dammit! The Devil! Why do humans always call out 'Oh my God' when terrified or shocked? All you're saying is, 'Now that I am in deep trouble, I am screaming for God to be my God right now.'"

While attempting to slow a rapidly beating heart, I say, "Just a bad nightmare to go with the nightmare of a bad day."

The mysterious voice announces, "Wrongful thinking dude, for I am not a dream, nightmare, or hallucination. I am greater than all those combined. I am Satan."

Every cell in my body demands I drop to the floor, land in a fetal position shouting, 'It's over.'

"Have you come to take my soul?"

"Maybe, but first I require you to write a book about me."

Bewildered, bothered, and four beats from a stroke, all I can say is, "A book? Why a book about you? And why me, why now?"

Before he could respond, it hit me. After three days and nights of worrying incessantly about what my medical test will reveal, I need this like General Armstrong Custer needed more Indians.

2

THREE THINGS YOU NEVER WANT TO HEAR

There are three things in life you never want to hear:

Will the defendant please rise?

If I can't have you, no one can.

You need to get your affairs in order.

Fortunately, and with no lack of effort on my part, I have not experienced such a day in court that I had to rise as a defendant. The second ominous declaration reminds me of that hot summer night by the lake with a full moon illuminating everything like a spotlight from a guard's tower during a prison break when I heard the finality of "If I can't have you no-one can" only to discover—much to my amazement—I could run on water. As to number three, something tells me that the subject of my affairs and order is about to be addressed.

Joined by an old nemesis dread, I wait for Dr. Andrew Grossman's office to call with the test results. There was so much lab work, it felt like I was being depleted of all bodily fluids. There it is again. Nervous nausea sourced from fear, rushing its way from my abdomen to constricting my throat, like an uncapped oil well gusher. With my luck, the message will be, "The Doctor needs to see you right away. And Mr. Largent, he asks that you pay in advance."

After three days of vainly trying not to worry and ongoing losing duels with Denial, the phone rings and the caller ID reads Dr. Grossman's office.

"Hello?" I timidly answer.

"Mr. Largent?" a female voice asks.

Lord, I want to say, 'Lady that's who you called' but since nurses are experts with sharp instruments I just say, "Yes."

"Your test results are in and the doctor wants to see you now."

Pleadingly I ask, "Can't you tell me over the phone?"

"No. He wants to see you right away," she says in a neutral distant tone that they must teach during the last semester of nursing school.

"I can be there at 2:00 PM today if he is available."

Much too quickly she says, "He will see you then."

Another ominous sign. Have you ever visited a doctor's office and heard, 'Come on in, the Doctor has been waiting for you'?

At least she didn't say I had to pay in advance.

WHILE DRIVING TO the doctor's office, a thought popped into my head—these last few days lots of thoughts have been popping into my head—it must have something to do with that awkward stage of premature death; not enough time to waste and too much time to think. There is no stopping these nagging questions in this bubble-wrapped brain. So many continuous, and sometimes nonsensical, questions—*"Do I have cancer? How long do I have to live? Since cattle only eat grass are they vegan?*—are as annoying as a middle child always asking, "Why? Why? . . . But why?"

At 44, I'm too old to fight, too young to get shot, and way too young to have cancer, if that's what it is.

These persistent mind-numbing headaches, sudden dizzy spells, and my daily nemesis, nausea, are the trifecta of trouble. I really shouldn't be driving.

Stop! Screeching smoking tires jerk me forward causing a death grip on the seat belt across my upper body coming within inches of tail-ending a black Ford F150 pickup truck stopped at a red light. Drivers all around me are glaring, and the guy in the pickup looks like he is debating with himself about jumping out of his truck and causing a re-experience of the tortuous journey through my mother's birth canal by grabbing both ears and jerking my terrified body through this half-recessed car window.

If Bubba does jump out of his big black truck, I know exactly what I am going to say. "Buddy, I am sorry but I am very ill and if you hit me—which you have a right to do—I will throw up all over you and that sleeveless tank top you so proudly wear." He will back off. How do I know? I successfully used that tactic while suffering a severe hangover at a desolate all-night diner in New Mexico. It was spontaneous then but planned now.

Praise the Lord, the light changed and everyone around me is blasting on car horns, saying 'move on A-hole.' All I could do was exhibit an exaggerated shrug of shoulders, hold up both hands to say, "I know; I am an idiot."

Doctor Grossman could have told me over the phone what my condition is or left me a post-it note on my front door. It's not like he's breaking up with me.

That's it, Max. Ward off bad news by blaming someone else's action—or lack of.

The drive to Grossman's office is 20 minutes and, at 1:30 PM there is little traffic on the back streets of West Nashville but I am driving like a hyper-vigilant stoner who doesn't want his being high on the highway to appear obvious all of which causes him to be obvious. Driving way too slow and continuously tapping the brake pedal, with a death grip on the steering wheel and eyes darting left and right for a safe place to pull over if I start to faint. I may not make it to being a senile old man but today I am driving like it. This is not fun and wouldn't be even if I were stoned.

Made it! I pull into the parking garage and drive down and down, going around and around, as if my life is literally plummeting down the drain. At last, the parking attendant is in his little shed, draped in an ill-fitting wrinkled uniform. With a slow movement enhanced by disinterest, he hands me a ticket. He doesn't even look up.

Damn, he can't look me in the eye. What does he know that I don't?

Whoa, I've got to quit this hyper-vigilant aimless thought pattern. No one knows or cares why I am here other than God, Dr. Grossman, and me. I am sure God is way too busy right now helping other undeserving drivers who are praying for a parking space close to the entrance.

I ease the dark blue Lexus RX350 SUV between the two white lines, bordered by a gray concrete column and a long white van capable of carrying The Mormon Tabernacle Choir cross country. After this misadventure, there is Uber in my future.

I ride the elevator to the eighth floor, disembark, and with steps of caution take an immediate left then a right, and arrive in the reception area. On arrival at the reception desk, Dr. Grossman's head nurse, Ms. Shelby, says, "Hi Max, go right in."

She doesn't say it with her usual warm smile and, like the parking attendant, avoids looking me in the eyes. Does she know what the parking attendant knows?

This is like you answered the doorbell and standing there are two big humorless looking guys with buzzed haircuts in ugly black suits announcing, "Hi. We are from the IRS and we're here to help." Not wanting to prolong her discomfort, I refrain from my usual glibness and say, "Thank you, Ms. Shelby."

While navigating the hallway to Dr. Grossman's office, I swear there is a chorus from the reception area singing, "Dead man walking, dead man walking here."

I find the office with his name on the small gray plaque, knock, and hear a low voice beckon, "Come in."

For twenty-three years Dr. Grossman has been my doctor and mentor. Though never expressed to him, I always wished he were my father or grandfather. How different life would have been if this good man had been in it from the beginning?

He stands to greet me but stays behind his desk. He extends his large right hand and gives me an economical half-smile and says, "Max, son, take a seat."

Son? He has never called me son. My emotions are on edge but, deep in the well of my longing to be loved by a parent, his salutation is comforting and alarming.

I sit like a puppy who cowers at every command. This giant of a man holds in his hand a file that determines my future, or lack thereof. We are on opposite sides of his sterile wooden desk with a clear glass top devoid of papers, giving the impression his desk is a barricade.

I feel like a guy just sentenced to the electric chair, who turns to his lawyer and asks, "Do you have any advice?" and his lawyer replies, "Whatever you do, don't sit down."

I know what you are thinking right now: He sure is silly for a guy in a serious situation. You're right, but being silly almost keeps me sane. Almost.

Doctor Grossman bows his head and looks at my file a bit too long.

It says I am six feet and half an inch tall, weigh 192 pounds, have dark receding hair, hazel eyes, olive complexion, and small scars over my right eye and on my chin. The mystery is what that file says about my future or lack of. I am as nervous as a long-tailed cat in a room full of rocking chairs.

He's hesitant to convey the file's contents.

Dr. Andrew Grossman is a mountain of a man, six foot three inches tall and a biscuit shy of 220 pounds. His snow-white hair crowns a monument of deep caring and intelligence. Those intense blue eyes seem to have x-ray vision. His hands are the size of an old catcher's mitt. When he takes your hand in his it feels like you just slid safely into home plate. He is sometimes gruff to prove a point, but as we say in the South, "The meat closest to the bone is the sweetest." And Dr. Grossman is closest-to-the-bone sweet.

There is moisture in his caring blue eyes. This is not good. He takes some time to compose himself then closes the file.

I am in a whiteout. The white walls, white window coverings cascading down to a cream-colored tile floor. Dr. Grossman's pale skin matches the white lab coat, even his pocket pens are white. All this white amplifies dark words.

"Max, son, you have brain cancer."

Fear has become reality.

Dr. Grossman's proclamation brings a flood of nausea from my rumbling stomach. Or is it panic? I repress this involuntary reaction so as not to be embarrassed in front of this gentle giant.

I have just been given a death sentence and I'm worried about being embarrassed. So what? No human wants to hear his or her days are numbered. Like, you are still in the game of life Max, but you can only play until half-time. My appearance is stoic, but inside I am like a gorilla in a hurricane. The fear is not so much in dying but that the last days will be the Four Horseman of the Apocalypse riding in on debilitating pain, persistent nausea, weakness, and dependence on the kindness of paid strangers for everyday bodily care.

At least I can now move past denial, like when a father notices his young son prefers his sister's dresses to jeans and he denies the inevitable until his friend, the President of the University, calls to tell him the good news—his son is being crowned Homecoming Queen.

The headaches, the dizzy spells, these are my dresses. Seeing Dr. Grossman's sad eyes, this is my homecoming.

I take pride in not having any emotional baggage, other than that denial thing. If you're going to have issues in life, denial is the best one, for it encompasses all other issues, without ownership. "You are passive-aggressive." Nope. "You have mommy issues." I don't think so! "You are afraid of commitment." No way. "You are in denial." Not even close. "Really?" Well, maybe.

"Max, son I'm afraid it's time to get your affairs in order."

There it is. The third thing in life you never want to hear. "Get my affairs in order?"

"Yes."

"Chronologically or alphabetically?" I blurt out.

Hey, don't blame me for this gallows humor of avoidance. It's the cancer, that's my excuse and I am sticking to it.

"Max," Dr. Grossman says, without smiling, "The brain tumor may have spread." His massive shoulders slump from the weight of his message.

"Is 'may' the significant word here?"

"No, I'm afraid the significant word is spread. Your tumor's a stage-four Glioblastoma."

My throat tightens and a cold sweat takes over my forehead. I focus on my breathing to stay present. Don't lose it, Max, not here, not with him. Face the facts. It is what it is and it's not what it's not. I now have a prognosis. Or is it a verdict? Disease means ill at ease, even if you can't spell or pronounce Glioblastoma.

Then I ask the scariest question anyone can ask. "How long do I have?"

The most important question in life is why we are here and the scariest is how long, do we have left to do it?

My doctor and friend of many years continues to look right at me and does not avert his sad eyes. You need to see Dr. Jackson Hamlett, an Oncologist at Vanderbilt University Hospital. I sent him the test results and he has agreed to see you. I am afraid without immediate care Dr. Hamlett says, 'You might live three months, with Surgery or Radiotherapy or Chemotherapy you might make it twelve to fifteen months.' I must warn you, Max, time is of the essence."

I lose it. "To hell with that! Why would I want to go through all that pain and misery to maybe live a few months?"

My aggressiveness startles him, the unwilling bearer of bad news. Damn it. Why did I raise my voice to this kind man who is just doing his difficult job? I try to make amends by saying, "I'm sorry."

"Why are you sorry?"

"I only have to hear that I'm dying once, but you have had to repeat this message many times."

His eyes widen and then he looks down to avoid acknowledging this moment of awareness. "How soon can you see Dr. Hamlett?"

He doesn't want to get into my feelings about him. He wants to stick with the facts. That's his coping strategy.

"May I let you know in a couple of days?"

Dammit, I will go but only so my dear friend and Doctor will feel like he has done everything he can for me. But it's a waste of time and I have no time to waste.

It turns out hearing you have terminal cancer is like going to jail for the first time; you know it's real when you hear the slamming of the doors of steel, I just heard my life slam shut. "I need time to think." Didn't I just say that?

He nods. "Let me know tomorrow. Whatever Dr. Hamlett recommends needs to be started immediately. I'm going to write you a new prescription for pain and one for steroids to help with the swelling. Do you have enough left over for the nausea and dizzy spells?"

"Yes, sir."

The big man comes around the desk and hugs me. Having never known a father's embrace, this touches my soul. In my head I hear, do anything but cry in front of him. Reluctantly, I end the hug and walk to the door worried that he is taking this with difficulty.

I turn to him. "Doctor, you forgot to tell me the most important thing."

With a puzzled expression, he replies, "What's that?"

"How is my cholesterol?"

He smiles and shakes his caring head.

3

LEAVING WITHOUT GRIEVING

To collect my discombobulated self, I lean against the wall outside his office—a zombie, oblivious to all surroundings. This trance takes me to an elevator mercifully devoid of another soul. I press the down button that will deliver me to the parking garage, P3. At last, something I can control.

Somehow, I find the car and sink into the driver's seat. With eyes closed, chin slumped to my chest, these tired hands have a white-knuckle grip on the black leather-wrapped steering wheel, feebly trying to hold onto life.

Breathe, Max. Holding your breath is not going to prolong life. The doctor's words keep running on a continuous loop: "Brain cancer. Stage-four Glioblastoma. Get your affairs in order."

After what must have been twenty or so minutes I slowly back out of the parking space and note the large white van is still there. Reaching the parking attendant's shed I remember the ticket which is still in my shirt pocket. I roll down the window and hand him the stub which states in black ink the car has been here an hour and sixteen minutes.

Sounding surprised, he blurts out, "They didn't validate your parking ticket?"

Taking a deep breath I say, "My bad. I forgot to give it to them, there were a few other things on my mind."

I hand him a twenty, "Keep the change." Pulling away not caring what his response may be.

Now, whom do I go to that will validate my life?

I just want to go home and sleep.

At least it can't get any worse.

4

YOU HUMANS ARE CREATING HELL ON EARTH

"Largent, did you go back to sleep?"
My eyes dart around the bedroom for evidence that this voice is real while hoping to God it's not.

"No, I was in deep thought on why you want a book."

"To save the world before it goes totally dark, and I am out of a job."

That impales me deeper on his pointed spike of terror. To try and clear a muddled head, I stumble to stand. The hardwood floor feels cool to my bare feet so I must be awake. With the caution of a Cat Burglar without the coordination, I make my way to the den. Sensing a dizzy spell, I grasp the arm of the couch. Rhett looks at me with concern as I fall onto the couch. Holding an aching head with both hands while almost wishing that in my terrible 20s there was a partaking of the hard drugs to be able to blame his voice on those induced flashbacks. Let's get this right. The Devil, the demon of darkness, wants to save the world in a book of all things—written by me. Miss Garvin, my high school English teacher, must be spinning in her grave. She would wag her bony finger at me and sternly say, "Maxwell, you have a vivid imagination; hopefully, you can put it to good use someday besides trying to make the girls giggle." Little did Miss Garvin know that my joy in life was the sound of a female's laughter.

"Forgive my play on words, but how in the hell can the Devil save humanity? I thought you wanted to destroy the world?"

"Listen, Largent, this is important. If humanity stays on its present path, it will no longer exist, end of the road, lights out, total darkness. The party is over. Then I will cease to exist. So will God."

"You want to save the world to save yourself?"

"I was kicked out of Heaven because I wouldn't bow down to humans and I told God, 'Humans were not worthy of your love or free will.' Humans have spent centuries proving me right. I love playing this game—I call it a game with God—on who can get the most souls. In this century, and the last, you people have gone bat-shit crazy and are proving my point. Too well, might I add. Humans are taking away my most perverse pleasure of leading the world astray. Perverse pleasure. Has a nice ring, don't you think?"

"When there is an agreement by all parties," I say.

"What are you? A lawyer?"

I am just a few weeks from dying and now spending precious time irritating Satan. Crazy is as crazy does.

He continues. "The human race is acting more like me without me and taking away all my significance."

"Whoa! Aren't you responsible for wars, bigotry, hate, pain, and pretty much all the world's wickedness?"

"Just because I thrive on such and promote those wonderful

situations, it is the human race with your free will who today take all that to the extreme and then try to blame me. The world today subscribes to 'love thy neighbor as thyself as long as thy neighbor looks and believes as thyself.' Even I couldn't make that up."

This is chilling my soul. I feel like a hostage negotiator who just realized he is the hostage.

"That's why you, Max Largent, are going to write this book. In today's world, all you self-loathing dumb-asses with all their religious and political wars, bigotry, and abuse, even going so far as selecting leaders not because they are competent but because they're haters like themselves. The world today is messed up and getting worse. You people are mucking with my entire purpose for being."

"What is your purpose for being?" I ask, stalling but also wanting to know the answer.

He shouts, "One more time, Largent! My purpose is to prove to God that most humans are not worthy of his love and grace and I can get more souls than he does.

His voice becomes deeper and more sinister. "I don't want all the souls. There's no fun in that. If the world stays on this present path of darkness through ignorance, evil and apathy there will be no place for God's light, it will lead to the end of the world. Game over, the final bell will have rung, the fat lady will have sung or whatever cliché your feeble minds need to understand."

I ask with caution, "You're going to save mankind so you can take their souls?"

"Close. But I don't want all of them. My book will be for people like you—not all bad, but on the edge of going to Hell due to your ignorance and apathy. You folks are lightweights to me and not as much fun to torture. The 'C' students of life, too unenlightened to go to Heaven and, by default, I must take them. With this book, I will open their closed eyes of avoidance and expel them to Heaven and make more room for my valedictorians of true evil."

"Are you saying, 'I am dimwitted and unenlightened?'"

"Max, if you don't like the peaches, don't shake the tree. Write the book; maybe even you will learn something that will keep your sorry ass out of Hell. Maybe."

"Whoa, dude! At this moment I may be scared and dying but the heck with you. This is not a way to get someone to write a book."

"Here is something you never thought you would hear the Devil say. Sorry."

"Really?"

"No!" He scoffs. "Write the damn book but don't put anything in it about me saying 'I'm sorry.'"

"Of course not. Besides, who would believe it?"

"Look Max, focus and try to understand. A world of people must change their ways soon because it's getting overcrowded here in Hell with all the unenlightened."

With that dark picture, I try to fall asleep worrying if I am that unenlightened.

5

WHAT DO YOU SAY, HEMINGWAY?

I can't sleep for fear of not waking up. Looking out the bedroom window at 1:20 AM, it's as dark as a Pawn Broker's heart.

A restless Rhett, sleeping at the bedroom threshold, murmurs short yelps. He must be dreaming of uncaught rabbits and uncatchable cars. I want to trade places with him.

With the tempo of a snail, I slide out of bed wearing nothing but lounge pants and this extra-large headache. I glance back at the mattress and am pleased to find there are no snail tracks.

Rhett stirs, stands, shakes off his dream and escapes through the open kitchen door for an early morning relief session. I consume three Advil pills because two won't do. I don't like the pain pills the doctor prescribed, they are supposed to be 'mild', but they still cause an irritable digestive system.

I make it to the office chair, sit, and lay warm hands over sore eyes while counting three long, slow breaths.

"Pay attention Largent."

"Attention to what?"

"I am going to make you famous. Some will say notorious."

"Don't want no part of being famous and I have already been notorious."

He chuckles, "That's right, that six-week marriage to a celebrity, your fifteen minutes of fame."

Ignoring the reference to what Andy Warhol said about "everyone has 15 minutes of fame," as mine turned out to be 15 minutes of shame.

"So, what are you going to do to me that hasn't been done? Get me to jump off the Empire State building with a sheep under one arm and a chicken under the other?"

"I love how your humor shines through your terror. That's one of the reasons I chose you out of all the souls who have chosen me."

My heart's beating like a heavy metal drummer on industrial-strength drugs. The Devil says. "I have chosen him." Chosen to go to Hell? This can't be true.

"Why do you say that?"

"It's an interesting story Max. A 44-year story called 'Your Life' that we will get into later, but for now I am offering you a potential way to escape my, shall we say, 'warm' company for eternity."

"How?"

"What the hell! Did you forget? Is it the brain tumor or the shock of learning about it that is causing you to make me repeat what I want—no, what I demand—that you write a book about me and today's crazy world."

"A book? I am not a writer."

"There you go again, that lame excuse all you humans use when you don't follow your natural desires and gifts. Those repeated lame excuses, I am not educated, I never had the opportunity, I am not good enough. It is never about excuses; it's about fear over passion. Look at those that didn't make it as a singer or actor. Did they want to sing or act for the joy of it, or did they just want to be rich and famous? Such limited awareness leads to a life controlled by fear of failure.

You are a writer, mostly in your head. You love to tell stories, you wrote poetry that was never shared, and you have kept a journal for years all the while hoping no one ever sees it so they can't judge you. You won't acknowledge it, but you are a writer. Can you write a declarative sentence?"

Taken back that he knows about my insecurities, I say, "Yes."

"That's a start. Tell my story the best you can and get an excellent editor, then you are a writer. Not a great one, but hey, Hemingway is dead so he's out and lucky for me you will be dead soon."

"What has my imminent death got to do with it?"

"I want an author who will not be around after the book is published so the world's focus will be on what I have to say. People do love to find someone to hate so they don't have to face their truth.

"You are lucky, Largent. An artists' too soon of a demise can be a great career move. Look at Elvis and Michael Jackson."

"Well, so far I have outlived Elvis by two years and eaten almost as many bacon cheeseburgers."

"Stay on point," he commands.

On point? I wish someone would point the way out of these conversations.

"This book you want me to write, it will have to be short; I have a stage four brain tumor."

The voice says, "I know, but guess what? I don't care."

"Also, it will take too long. My lips move when I read thus editing will take longer than I have to live."

"Write the book and find an editor."

This S.O.B. won't buy any excuse I am selling. "I won't do it. I want to enjoy what little time I have left."

"Not to worry. It's a quick assignment, and you'll get to die as a famous writer. You've always wanted to be a writer, but your fear of failure or—even worse—success got in the way. I like that you will be gone soon and won't be around for the backlash."

"What backlash?" This demon knows his book is going to be controversial and upset people. Maybe that's why he wants it?

"I hate to whine, but why me?"

Why whine? I am only sitting here perspiring in a stifling room and trapped in a dialogue with the Devil. Lord help me.

I struggle to open the window next to the desk to let the cool air in and to have a quick exit. But to where, the backyard?

"Max, you're the perfect choice; you're a charismatic enigma. You're one of those classic creative types—crazy, unpredictable, and always coloring outside the lines.

"I can see it now," he says. "All over the world mass burnings of bonfires fueled by this book. These fires of contempt will be sourced by ignorance and fear sparked by extremists in organized, and not so organized, religions and sects."

"Is this to be my posthumous reputation, uniting crazy-ass extremists in bonfires?"

He breaks my train wreck of thoughts.

"Don't flatter yourself, radicals don't need an excuse to flaunt their ignorance. But as they say in the hood, 'Dude, I like your 'tude,' as in attitude."

There is a delight in his voice, even pride.

"If you can't tell by now, I love religious extremists. Throughout the history of the world I, the Devil, have been the biggest fan of fanatics. They all believe their way is *the only way*, carrying with it the obligation to murder all souls who suggest otherwise.

That includes some so-called 'good Christian churchgoers'—of the 'if you don't love Jesus you can go to Hell' type. They're among my favorites because they are so blinded by their views that they don't realize if someone doesn't believe in their Jesus, they sure aren't going to believe in their hell. Put that in the book. It will drive them crazy. I love nothing more than angry fanatics for they will be keeping me company for a terribly long time, and I do mean terrible.

"You see, fanatics—religious or political—all have a deep-seated fear that they are wrong, or worse, found out. Rather than confronting their fear of not being 100 percent correct 100 percent of the time they speak out against others. These angry people are mean, cruel, and judgmental because they sense a part of themselves in others that they are too afraid to acknowledge. I thrive on these people for they embody my three wise men of fear.

"Let this book give the fanatics and fear mongers more ammunition to end up in Hell. Let God have those who are intelligent enough *not* to force their beliefs on others. Don't need them. Don't like them."

"Then you don't need my sorry soul?"

"That is up to you."

6

TO BE IN HAWAII

Awake, my tongue is so dry it feels like I have spent the night licking pool tables.

"But, and a big but it is, I am a winner because here is a new day announced by sunlight peeking through the window to cast a welcoming glow to say, "Welcome to life."

Thank you, Lord.

While trying to sit up, dizziness takes control. I stay down. Did I dream there was more dialogue with the Devil, or was it a nightmare?

With a caution that would make a burn patient proud, I rise and move to the kitchen. One cup of hot coffee is good, two is better.

Even with caffeine, there is still confusion. Yes, I drove to Dr. Grossman's office. No, I cannot recall a thing about the return trip. Driving in shock is not a recommended form of transport. I am not sure of much these days. There is certainty in this: Future driving and the independence it brings are subject to moods—and meds.

I can't stop thinking about what little time there is left on this round rock called earth. I must die in Hawaii; it is my spiritual home of serenity. A personal Mecca where the totems of nature and the slow pace of life allow the grace of living in the moment. The Islands of Hawaii bring into focus a strong connection to Spirit, God, and the Universe, supporting the belief there is a source greater than just us, mere mortals. In my present state, I am betting on it.

Whatever definition is used for God is correct for that believer. I have a sense that the Great Creator does not care for labels, or such, just a little acknowledgment when we are not asking for something.

In Hawaii, there is less reaction to cell phones, emails, newspapers, and that ever-present downer 24-hour TV news. This respite from negativity allows me an audience with my Higher Self to be grateful and request a miracle, like a full-time love, a better job, more hair, and that little please-cure-my-cancer thing. I envy those who find a quiet place in their minds to retreat from the everyday tribulations of life, be it Calcutta or Greenwich, Connecticut.

I have visited the Islands five times, exploring Kauai, Maui, Oahu, and the Big Island twice, once staying for four months. The first visit was nine years ago after closing a real estate transaction that facilitated the funds to go as far west as possible without a passport. There was a knowing on that sunny initial visit, that if blessed with will and grace this land of *Aloha* Spirit would be my final "departure lounge." The beauty of the Island, its blue rhythmic ocean, and laid-back locals soothed my soul. Obviously, you don't need to go to an island in paradise to connect with Spirit. However, when you are immersed in natural beauty, perfect weather, and a nonreactive lifestyle you live life in three-quarters time. As was explained on my first visit, "Slow down, dude, here in the Islands, *mañana* does not mean tomorrow, it means not today."

In Hawaii and its soulful stillness Spirit finds you. But if that doesn't work, try Hoboken, New Jersey or anywhere that helps you focus inward and go deeper.

Hawaii has the cleanest air, as it is the farthest landmass from any other point in the world. I knew that I would be retiring there; I just didn't know it would be so soon and would be a full-blown final retirement. I am not delusional enough to think that running away to paradise will buy me more time on earth. But God, if you are listening, I am open to that if it is painless.

Typical human. Putting conditions on a miracle.

Now to make plans for my last road trip. No need for shiny blue and gold tour jackets with lettering that says, Max Largent's Final Tour. Besides, I doubt if TSA would let me through security much less on a plane wearing such a declaration of finality. The only scenario more problematic would be attempting to board my flight while wearing a parachute.

Another monkey mind moment where thoughts swing from one synapse to the other with no mental GPS.

How will my deathbed scene play out?

Maybe I will philosophize, like Voltaire. When a Catholic priest administering last rites asked the dying French philosopher, "Do you renounce Satan?" He replied, "Now is not the time to make new enemies." Nah, I will go out like the great philosopher Porky Pig, "That-that-that's all folks!"

For the moment, this gallows humor lifts my spirits while sliding down the slippery slope of a shortened life.

My biggest concern is finding Rhett a good home. When you have been given unconditional love, you want that entity, be it animal or human, to always be taken care of. I just don't know whom to ask.

As if to tell me not to worry, the big dog gets up from his bed and crosses the room to my chair. He nuzzles my leg, wags his bushy tail for the obligatory pat, and lies down so we are closer.

This dilemma is precipitated by the self-inflicted lifestyle of being a popular loner. No real family, one true friend, and a few acquaintances because being alone was preferable, except for Rhett and he doesn't talk much. I am such a loner I would get arrested for loitering in Times Square on New Year's Eve.

Here comes fear. Out of the blue, it appears in the form of recalling that psychiatrist Elisabeth Kübler-Ross listed in her five stages of grief: denial, anger, bargaining, depression, and acceptance. I'll add a sixth to her list: Scared out of your feeble mind.

Instead of letting fear take control, I will focus on the business side of dying. The need to set up a fund for Rhett's care and name a Power of Attorney to pay for the final days of kindness provided by strangers. There is only one person to ask, my true friend, Billy Bob Baker, the mover and shaker.

I trust Billy Bob to the point I'd play poker with him over the phone.

"What cards are you holding, Billy Bob?"

"Three aces."

"Dad-gum. I only have three Kings."

I can't ask Billy Bob to take Rhett. Billy Bob has lived all his life as a bachelor in Houston, Texas and he is skittish around anything with more than two legs. Not everyone in Texas is a cowboy or wants to be. As a good friend, he can help with the dreary financial details of dying by arranging payments from my bank account for nursing care, hospice, and burial. My burial will be simple: no memorial or funeral, just cremation and scattering of the ashes—I was about to say my ashes but no need to personalize this so soon. Hey, do not hate the player, hate the game.

Rhett raises his head, turns, and looks up with concern. He knows.

I read that the attendance at your funeral will *not* be determined by how much you were liked and loved or whether you lead an exemplary life, but whether or not it rains.

Even on a sunny day, the best chance I have for a well-attended funeral is if there were door prizes, an open bar, and the Dallas Cowboy Cheerleaders.

Need to remind Billy Bob, that's not in the budget but it would put the fun in *fun*eral.

7

WE DROPPED THE CHARGES

Nothing is more worrisome than an angry Devil. A dark menace I can only hear and see flashes of. He is in my home and head, uninvited.

He is correct. This world today is messed up. Take the evening news. Out of thirty minutes, twenty-nine are filled with reports of violence, mayhem, and lying politicians, then one minute of a singular feel-good story to keep us coming back. Corporations selling fear for profit.

It is an easy sell for all those scared people looking for someone else to blame for their misery.

I wish there was someone else to blame for this misery while prone on this couch with a queasy gut and a head that is throbbing with more pressure than the *Titanic* on the bottom of the Atlantic. Just a few months ago it was feeling titanic with physical strength and a future, now I am sunk. If only there were five minutes of a welcomed distraction. It would be a momentary relief to get a call from a 1-800 number asking, "If there is any interest in aluminum siding for my brick home." Anything to change the subject.

HE'S BACK AND I suspect he's not here to talk about aluminum siding. He speaks. "In previous centuries, light sped through the cracks of dark times and humans evolved as a civilization. As I have said. In this century the world is headed to Armageddon. I thrive in dark times but you people today with your instant messaging, social media, and everyone with a phone or computer believing they have the right to spew their venom and falsehoods. All under the phony flag of 'It's my right.' You humans today are turning the world into *total* darkness.

"Without light in the world, there is no rhythm or rhyme to the dance called life. No light, no life, no God, no Devil; this is humanity's last call."

"Aren't you a bundle of joy?" I utter sarcastically.

"There will be no joy in those dark times, even for me."

I tell him about the dream. "One recurring dream that haunts me—I do the deed of dying and meet God at one of the twelve gates of pearl and she says, 'My child, what were you thinking all those 44 years? Life is just a dance. You were so busy trying to master the perfect steps, you couldn't feel the rhythm.'

"What could I do?' I reply. She responds, 'You could have been still and felt my love and life's rhythm. To your detriment, you got caught up in the mental distractions of negative thinking.'"

"Largent in these dreams of yours, what is the difference between God's rhythm and life's cycle?"

"As I see it God's rhythm is an easy waltz in three-quarter time, flowing back and forth. Life's rhythm is like break dancing with bad knees. You love the beat and the loud pulsating music, but every move is painful."

"Max, out of curiosity, if by some slim chance you do get to Heaven, what is the first thing you want to hear God say?"

"We dropped the charges."

ALTHOUGH MY HEAD is throbbing, I figure if he won't leave me alone, I may as well get him to explain a few things. "So what if you, the Devil, ceased to exist?" I ask.

"You are so naive," he says, in a disgusted tone. "I will always exist as long as there is fearful mental chatter. Thoughts and words create; that's one of the reasons I hate meditation. Without words or thoughts my message can't get through. I can't paint a masterpiece of misery on a blank canvas. I exist because people are always thinking and believing the worst about each other and themselves. I survive on their pitiful, painful thoughts."

Now I'm alert and hopeful. "Are you telling me if I meditate, creating a blank canvas, I can get you out of my aching head?"

"You will be safe while meditating but open those green eyes and I will be on you like black at midnight until you write my book."

"Okay, okay. I hear you. Now let me get my all-encompassing blanket. I am almost as cold as your words."

"Enjoy that cold while you can, Max. If you don't finish my book, you'll be here with me where there is no conditioned air, at least not to anyone's liking." He laughs.

I think, *what an asshole*.

"I heard that."

Now I get to grin.

From the bedroom closet I retrieve a beautiful, vibrant red and blue wool Wellington Blanket, like the American Indians of the old West would have made if they had invested in the machinery. I am going to meditate in hopes that it will relieve some of the physical pain and stop this dialogue with you know who. With a blanket bringing welcomed warmth to my shoulders and back, I sit in the leather recliner and close my eyes.

I am a ten- to twenty-minute meditator, not that this worried mind is blank all that time. Even when just focusing on my breath some uninvited thoughts still barge in. In such moments it is best to treat my mind like a small child who has wandered off a garden path; then gently guide it back onto the path of peace.

This cozy quilt was given to me by a wonderful young lady named Frances who was making her angry exit. "This is for your cold heart."

Frances was so worked-up about our breakup, I had to remind her to take her umbrella. I wanted to say, "Here, take your umbrella, we have nothing more to weather." But even a fool, such as I, is wise enough to keep his tongue in place and mouth shut while still in possession of teeth and consciousness during any occasion of a woman's anger.

It's easy to say now that I was doing her the favor of her young life. She was several years younger and had a view of the future I couldn't share, like having children and barbecues in the backyard. She deserved to have those experiences, as she came from a wonderful loving family, but I had no reference point to relate to my ability at being a father or husband. Also, I don't grill. That of course is an excuse, but what is not an excuse is she would have emotionally drowned in my sorrow of the past. Even if she had the desire to learn to swim in those muddled waters, I truly cared for her and couldn't ask her to endure it. At that moment all she wanted from me was to have the last word. My parting gift to her.

Besides, I liked the blanket.

Covered by the warm gift, I ease back in the recliner, trying not to think about the Devil or his book. The writing desk is clear and uncluttered, too bad the same can't be said about my mind.

Fifteen minutes later. "Here's Johnny!" I shout, thinking of the movie *The Shining* and how I must resemble the wild-eyed manic look of Jack Nicholson's character as he splinters open the door with an ax.

"What?" replies the uninvited guest.

"Never mind. Tell me, Demon of Demons, what do you know about Enlightenment?"

"Excellent question. Messages of enlightenment have been available for thousands of years and look where it has got the world? My followers have twisted messages of enlightenment in the Torah, the Bible, the Koran, and countless self-help books for their own profit, which, might I add, good job."

"They put the profit in prophet." I smirk. Before he could respond I ask, "Why, with this book are we *now* going to believe the Devil?"

"I don't need anyone to believe anything. Remember, I got more souls today than ever before, so I am trying to weed out those like you who may go to Hell for eternity out of ignorance and apathy. I need the space for the truly evil who are growing in amazing numbers.

"I want the souls who live on the border between Heaven and Hell to start thinking. That way those who have arrived here of their own accord will have no excuse for their damnation."

"It's those folks who never think for themselves—just about themselves—who create my havoc in the world. Have you ever known an atheist that murdered because someone *didn't* believe the way they do?

"Heaven has non-believers and Hell has so-called true believers. It's all about how you lived. Those who say you are limited to believing one way are saying, 'Everyone has to believe my way.' They cry 'religious persecution' not because they can't worship as they please but because you don't worship as they do.

"You can imagine the shock of some of those righteous soldiers when they see Atheists march into Heaven and they can't. Aghast, they ask in wonder, 'How can these nonbelievers enter the Kingdom of Heaven and we can't?'

"God responds, 'Because they did *not* kill anyone in my name.'"

I reply, "There are going to be some other surprised folks if I arrive in Heaven. I can see it now, some of the souls I knew on earth will be shocked—yes shocked—to see me. 'Holy cow! There is Max Largent. He drank, cussed, chased women, gambled, didn't go to church except during weddings, funerals, and bingo night and that wild man is here in Heaven? Shaken and confused they will be left wondering why and how. Disappointed that all those good times they passed up were for naught."

The Devil says, "They won't be as surprised as the so-called Spiritual do-gooders who end up keeping me company. They speak of their love of God but mistreat her children and her planet earth." He laughs with that haunting voice that sounds like it comes from the bottom of a deep dark well.

Shuddering under the blanket and thinking, I should ask Frances to borrow her umbrella; I have a lot to weather.

8

BILLY BOB BAKER, THE MOVER AND SHAKER

Did I wake up or come too? This confusing condition takes me back to Sunday mornings during my twenties. In those wild days that question was asked and never answered with certainty. Lo and behold dawn is breaking and the soft illumination of early light flows through the window, highlighting sheer curtains and settles with ease on the bedroom floor. God's gentle reveille, the French word for wake up. In this early morning state, I lie here in silence absorbing the calm and being aware that there are not too many of these moments left for grace and gratitude.

With a sudden jolt, Rhett lands on the bed, using his bushy tail to drum the white duvet into submission and to let me know he is excited to go out, no matter how serene the moment.

A liberated Rhett rushes outside to do his business and frolic in the yard while I fill his food bowl.

There was oatmeal for dinner last night because I like it; it is easy on my stomach, and it is all I have. For breakfast, it is strong black coffee, oatmeal, and for dessert is dry toast.

There is a phone message. Dr. Grossman's office has called in three prescriptions to Walgreens Pharmacy for a stronger pain pill—praise the Lord—and a liquid something for nausea plus more steroids. My head is aching to the point that it hurts to blink. Although I suffer in silence, Rhett can tell something is wrong as he leaves his bowl of food to come over to the kitchen counter and lay at my feet. He looks up and there is a concern in his caring chocolate brown eyes.

I double the mild pain pills on hand and ease the way to a most prized possession—the throne of a brown leather recliner, that has followed me from the last two residences. It is on this throne that I have presided over the most important decisions one can make: Do we have trade with Red China, should we raise corporate taxes, and do I order a pizza with or without extra cheese? Heavy is the head that wears the crown of Village Idiot. It is in this comfort zone of a throne that I have watched bad movies with car chase scenes and frontal nudity, sporting events, read, slept, and meditated.

After 20 minutes of keeping my eyes closed and not moving, the pain pills finally kick in. Now to try and do what I don't want to do.

The emotions of what must be done force a deep inhalation and a long exhalation. I slowly speed dial my best friend.

Billy Bob Baker, the blond-haired, blue-eyed mover and shaker who can charm birds out of trees and sell humidity to Houston.

Billy Bob's got a devil-may-care attitude and a heart as big as Texas. He knows all the pretty women in Houston plus more than a few in Dallas and Austin. I would not be surprised if he didn't have a female friend or two in Pecos, Texas. Billy Bob's attraction to women knows no geographical limits. What's most impressive is they all like him, even the ones he used to date, a rare talent.

I once asked Billy Bob, "Have you dated every pretty girl in Houston?"

"No," he replied, "but I did date their Mamas."

AS FOR THE women in my life, I see no need to burden them with my demise. Truth be told, I am avoiding the well-intended but annoying Belles of the South heavy hair syndrome.

Carrie Fisher, who had seen her share of insincere sympathy, once said, "The heavy hair syndrome occurs when you encounter a female acquaintance after bad news. They tilt a perfectly coiffed head as far as they can, as if their hair is way too heavy on that side and whine, 'Are you okay?'"

How could I not reply? "No, I am not okay! I am going to die in three months and football season starts in four."

Bless their hearts.

I know one thing for certain. Billy Bob will be kind and understanding. His loving Mama instilled in him a determination to always show kindness to others. I never met Billy Bob's mama but all the wonderful stories her proud son shared made me wish I had. Like Billy Bob, I am an only child, but I have always been envious of his loving upbringing.

His Mama would say, "Now Billy Bob, when you do something nice for someone there's a deposit made in your name in Heaven." Thus, Billy Bob Baker has a permanent preponderance to please. Very few people have an account in Heaven's kindness bank as large as Billy Bob Baker's.

Judy answers the phone. Judy 'the Cutie' is Billy Bob's faithful and sweet assistant. She has known Billy Bob longer than anyone.

They met as students at the University of Texas. They weren't in attendance together all those years. As Judy tells it, "Billy Bob was at UT when I got there, and he was there when I left."

His major was campus lifestyles.

Billy Bob likes to brag that he and Judy had lots in common—they both received just one B their entire college career. I remind Billy Bob, "I am sure you were a whole lot prouder of your B than Judy was of hers."

Billy Bob Baker is a Texas oilman in the sense that he gets landowners to lease their mineral rights to oil companies, where his talent for charming birds out of trees comes in handy. As J. Paul Getty said, "The meek shall inherit the earth but not its mineral rights."

After a quick and genuine "so glad to hear your voice" from both of us, Judy connects me to Billy Bob.

"Maxwell Largent indeed! How are you? We haven't talked in a month of Sundays." His usual exaggerated upbeat high-energy welcome.

"Billy Bob, there are three things in this world I don't like—cauliflower, bigots, and my current situation."

Sensing the seriousness in my voice Billy Bob's speech pattern slows from a hundred miles-per-hour to school zone slow. "What is it, Buddy?"

Bad news is like a shot of cheap Tequila; it should be taken straight and quick, so I say, "I have terminal cancer."

Billy Bob takes a long pause. I've never known him to take a pause, much less a long one. Stop the press. Bless his big ol' Texas heart, he's at a loss for words.

"How bad?"

Not wanting to add to his unease, I don't ask, "Buddy, what part of terminal don't you understand?"

Instead, I attempt to level things out a little and say, "The Doctor suggested I not buy any green bananas."

There is no laugh. "What can I do? I can be on the first thing smoking." Always his first response to an emergency or a party.

Now it is my turn to not know what to say. I struggle for a moment. "Sorry to spring this on you, but you are too far away for me to take for a candlelight dinner to break it gently."

"Max, this is serious."

"You're telling me, Buddy." Rhett runs to the picture window and starts barking. I stay seated to save strength for our conversation. Rhett's quick retreat from the window indicates it is a trespassing squirrel.

"Is that the world-famous Rhett?"

"Sure is." I am appreciative of the break to catch my breath before I say the words that have rarely parted my lips to anyone. "I need your help."

"Anything."

"There are a few things you could do that would ease my mind. First, please don't tell anyone."

No answer, then a low, "Okay," like he is thinking of whom he would tell.

"Second, if I haven't found a good home for Rhett before I ride off into the sunset, please make sure that happens."

"Done."

"Next, I need you to be the executor of my limited resources to make sure all my expenses for end-of-life care are paid out from my bank account."

"Done."

For a man who loves to talk he sure is to the point. Shock can do that.

"Last thing is, I would like my ashes laid upon the waters of the Mauna Kea Beach on the Big Island of Hawaii. I am going to try and get there and pay someone to lay ol' Max's remains on the waters before it is time to make an ash out of myself. In the event that's not possible please see that it gets done."

"Buddy, it will be my honor. You always loved Hawaii. I never understood how a Tennessee boy could love the tropics so much."

"Why would you?" You never go outside your zip code unless it is to find oil in the ground. There I experience a natural flowing inner peace and as the folks in Japan say about a massage, 'peace washes over me like 10,000 gentle waves.'"

I pause for a moment then add, "I am sorry to hit you with this and at the same time ask for favors."

"Max, please don't say that. I will do whatever you need and if you had asked someone else, I would have never forgiven you."

"By the way, do you know anyone in Houston in the book publishing business?"

"Yes," he says, "I know an agent and a marketing person for self-publishing. Why?"

"It is too weird to get into now, but I may send you a manuscript for publication. Assuming I have the time and energy to finish such a project."

"Consider it done, my friend."

I say, "Gotta go before we both say something so sweet it will question our sexual preferences."

"Nothing wrong with being gay," he says, "but as you, my dear friend, have been telling me for years, if we had put as much energy into making money as we had the romantic ties that bind we would have made Jeff Bezos look like a pauper."

To try and lighten the moment, I ask, "Are you dating anyone special?"

"Maxwell." He calls me Maxwell when he wants to make a

point. "You know anyone I date is special and that I would rather be number two to ten than number one to one."

"True," I reply. "You ever notice when there is talk of romance it is 'ties that bind and wedlock'?"

We both laugh, a wonderful reward from my kind-hearted friend. Then he turns serious.

"Max, there aren't enough words in the world to tell you how sorry I am. Be assured, you will not go through this alone. Promise that you will let me know how it's going and that you won't do anything rash without talking to me."

"What? Do something rash like overdosing on cauliflower?"

"Yea, something like that."

Sensing we have said all we can say for now, I close with, "Love you, Buddy." Over the years the very few times the word love comes up between us we always end it with 'Buddy' to man it up. Yes, men do have unfounded heterosexual fears based on unwritten rules. As in, two guys never sit next to each other at a movie. Ball games are okay but in a dark movie theater, there is always an empty seat between you. Two guys never go to the Symphony together unless they are performing, and they never ever feed each other at a restaurant.

"Love you too, Max."

We hang up—maybe for the last time.

Just thinking about Billy Bob lifts my heavy spirits. I call Rhett, who follows me into the bedroom. His nails click out a rhythmic cadence on the hardwood floor. Interesting how I am noticing the little sounds and sights that before were just background noise and passing glances.

Cauliflower, Bigots and Cancer. While laying down with closed eyes, it comes to me there is one more thing I don't like besides Cauliflower, Bigots and Cancer . . . making my dear friend sad.

9

IS GOD A WOMAN?

There are questions I have of the Devil—whether I write his book or not. Like why he wants a book that he believes will slow down humanity on its mad dash toward total darkness.

But why do I? Why would I write a book about the Devil? Not for the money; I will not be here to spend it. Not for fame or notoriety, I have already told him that. To hold a mirror up to the world in these crazy times? In that case, the book should be titled, *Bassackwards Insight for Forward Thinking People*. To mess with the heads of the so-called self-righteous who consciously—or not—do the Devil's work? I like the thought of that.

He is making it personal by holding up a mirror to the cracks in my life. Maybe as I get farther along in these conversations and reflections, I will figure this out. Is it to cover as many bases as possible for the afterlife? Elvis Presley sang Gospel songs, studied the Bible, and sometimes wore a Star of David, because, as he said, "I don't want anything to happen on a technicality."

I may write his book, for there would be nothing worse than having to reply to being asked, "Why are you here in Hell for eternity?" with "I had writer's block."

BACK AT THE desk, a life-long question pops up like burnt toast in an overheated toaster.

"Is God a man or woman?" I ask.

"God is transgender."

"Say, what? Are you telling me God can't go to the restroom in North Carolina?"

"No, wise ass. God transcends gender, for God is energy."

"What are you?" I ask with hesitance.

"I am dark, demonic, disingenuous, dangerous energy and I like it."

I think, why me? As Dorothy Parker once lamented, 'What fresh hell is this?'

"Okay?" I say, as in not okay. "Then why has God always been called he?"

"Who wrote all the early religious books?" the Devil asks.

"Men."

"There you go. A bunch of He's. Antediluvian religious scholars were not going to give away their power and call God a She. Keep the sexes separate. Don't allow women to learn to read. Humans are a soul with a body; thus, souls are energy."

"If we are all energy then I am energy, Rhett is energy, and you are energy, what's the difference?"

He laughs and says, "I have more fun, I don't blame others, and hardly ever wag my tail."

"Do you ever tell the truth?" I ask.

"Only when the truth hurts. Like a politician, I would never ever lie unless it's absolutely necessary."

'Which is?"

"Always."

"What about loved ones that have passed or that come to us in dreams?"

"That's wishful remembrance."

"What about the ones who believe that God is within us?"

"You mean, 'Be still and know that I am God?'"

"Yep, those folks."

"That works for them. But the opposite is also true: 'Be fearful and know I am the Devil.'"

"What is the true religion, the true God?"

"You are asking the Devil?"

You're my only audience now."

"Largent there are thousands of religions in the world, and some don't even use the word religion.

"Religion is from the Latin word *re-igare* meaning "to reconnect to the true self." Being Latin, it obviously doesn't encompass all faiths. The exciting news for me is that fewer people every day recognize themselves as being religious. The bad news is many of those still believe in God."

"Are you saying they don't feel the need for a middle-man to connect to God?"

"Ask them. All I am saying is what is true for anyone is true for them and everyone else should mind their own beliefs. What I am proud to say is, I am the true evil."

"That I believe. How about this: What religion is least represented in Hell?"

"Every race, color, creed, religion, and non-religion are well represented in Hell. I enjoy the negative, abusive, bigoted, and other charming wrongful actions of mean-spirited humans. But that doesn't mean I like them. I, the Devil, don't discriminate for I have never been prejudiced."

"You have never been prejudiced?"

"Of course not. I dislike everyone."

"And God loves everyone," I reply.

"That's her problem. I can tell you, in today's world God faces more disappointment than I do.

"I will give the readers a little hint. The more one is at peace on earth, the less chance that person will have the pleasure of my charming company," he says, laughing his scary laugh.

"Back to your question about true religion and true belief. Whatever is true for you, is true. Yes, there are false prophets but false to whom? So many fools get caught up in what is 'true,' as if life is a true or false quiz and they always must be right, or they have failed. Their beliefs turn rigid.

"Rigid thinking grounds them in ignorance and with my bellows of fear I stoke a fire of uncertainty reshaped and made stronger with a pounding hammer of anger that makes them malleable to my ways. Being incapable of adopting new ways of deepening one's righteousness can lead to rigor mortis of the soul."

Why am I listening to this? Pausing to look inward, what comes up is, when at death's door—and the door is ajar—there is a desperate need not to be wrong. Your head is on a swivel looking for confirming or disconfirming answers to everything. This is called the motivation to know before I go.

THE DISINGENUOUS DEVIL'S words are one-sided and self-serving, but what is true? True for you? True for me? Does it even matter?

The juvenile thinking that you will have plenty of time to get right with God is a fallacy of the foolish. I have been awarded an ominous heads up, a prize I would be glad to postpone for 40 or 50 years. Since my time here is now measured in weeks, I will continue to seek answers until death do I part.

As a seeker, I have experienced a Sweat Lodge, which meant

being hot, sweaty, and smelly with a bunch of moaning strangers. I attended a Yoga retreat where on the first day I got tendinitis, and by the fourth day was kicked out for smuggling in a cheeseburger. Thought of going to a Monastery in Big Sur California for a two-week retreat but couldn't get past the part in the brochure where you had to get up at 4:00 AM to meditate, clean bathrooms, and eat cold porridge. As a seeker I have learned that a spiritual experience is comparable to camping in the wild; you don't have to be miserable to enjoy nature or connect to God and you can still be a practicing carnivore.

I scan this Google brain for questions and try to play game show host.

"Is there anything I can wear, write, or recite to avoid going to Hell besides your book?" I ask the Devil.

"Why? Are you looking for a loophole?"

"Hey dude, I would wear a Star of David, a red dot on my forehead, a Saint Christopher's medal, and carry a dead black cat by its tail, if it kept me from joining your company."

"No totem is going to get you into Heaven, not even on a technicality."

I think, Sorry Elvis.

He goes on. "A Rabbi and a Priest are sitting in the front row of a boxing match. As the bell rings to start the fight one of the fighters makes the sign of the cross. The Rabbi turns to the Priest and asks, 'Does that sign thing help him win?' The priest replies, 'Not if he can't fight'."

CONTINUING, HE SAYS. "I don't desire the company of eighty-percent believers and twenty-percent seekers. They drive me crazy, always asking, 'Why?' like a middle child. Can't work with open-minded people, just when I have them in one of my dark philosophical corners, they use intellectual curiosity to shed light on a new way of believing. Spouting that 'There are no wrong answers, just wrong actions,' 'You can do anything you want as long as you don't hurt others' and how I hate that 'All religions are correct' crap.

HE IS IRKED. "A long time ago I asked God if Heaven had any perfect souls."

"Is that when She kicked you out?"

Not hearing an answer, I lay my head on crossed arms with eyes throbbing and ears buzzing.

As part of a determinative process as to whether to write his book, it intrigues me how the said book will be received.

"I'm glad I won't be around for the reaction to your book. There will be some scared and angry so-called true believers who will want to burn it. I hope they do, and they burn a million of them."

"Why do you want them to burn a million of my books?" he asks.

"To burn a million books, they have to buy them."

"Max, I am not in this for the money."

"Yes, but if I am going down in infamy for writing your account of today's world, I at least want a bestseller. Nothing worse than getting blamed for something you didn't enjoy."

"I like that, making important decisions based on your ego. You humans seldom disappoint the Devil."

"I disagree, Your Menace. There will be those seekers who will read this and gain insight on how to beat the Devil. Maybe the title should be *How to Beat the Devil and Have Fun While Doing It*."

Chuckling at my own words a serious question pops up. "As a child, I would hear, 'God will send you to Hell'."

"Jesus Christ, Abraham, the Prophet Muhammed, and in the name of Jerry Garcia and the Grateful Dead, have my disciples done such a good job that modern-day people still have not learned that God is a loving God and not a vengeful one? Why would She give free will then punish you for making wrong choices? Life is not a whack-a-mole.

Whoever says that to a child must enjoy scaring the bejesus out of them when putting them to bed making them repeat "If I should die before I wake, I pray the Lord my soul to take.' Then wonder why the little ones are wide-eyed, awake all night, and wetting the bed."

"After this book, lost souls will have no excuse for their subterfuge of avoiding the truth. I will tell them, 'No complaining. You had 2,000 years of spiritual teachings—and a book from me—so get your miserable selves down here and suffer for eternity.'"

Sliding into slumber, the last thought is. "Now I lay me down to sleep, I pray the Lord my soul to keep. Please!"

10

THE ONCOLOGIST

How badly do I *not* want to see the oncologist? I would prefer the misery of a three-day Bruce Willis Film Festival.

What can an oncologist say that would convince me to endure the pain and risk of brain surgery? Not to mention the unmitigated anguish of repeated chemotherapy treatments including having to spend more time in a hospital than a slick lawyer looking for new clients.

I am only going because of the promise made to Dr. Grossman, plus there is one question of importance that needs to be asked. It doesn't include time left on earth, pain factors, or how to say "Glioblastoma" cancer without someone responding "gesundheit." So, on this bright spring morning, with resurrecting colorful flowers and birds cheerfully serenading, Uber is taking Goober to the Vanderbilt Brain and Skull Center in West Nashville.

Didn't take pain meds this morning in case Dr. Jackson Hamlett wanted to ask me an important question like, "What's your name?"

This will be a quick visit so I can keep my word to Dr. Grossman and get an answer to a most perplexing question.

After a long walk that required following signs with arrows on gray walls and once stopping to ask directions, I find the Brain and Skull Center. It would say a lot about Vanderbilt Hospitals if they would have as their symbol a Skull and Cross Bones flag hanging over the lobby and Fun House mirrors at the exit causing your body to appear distorted like a Picasso painting to make you laugh while you are crying.

I check in at the large waiting room painted a soothing blue. Cushioned chairs with leather armrests are separated with glass side tables holding outdated Travel magazines for people who aren't going far. Floor-to-ceiling windows allow maximum natural light and give a clear view to Heaven. As I take a seat everyone in the reception area glances my way probably thinking, I wonder what he has and is he worse off than me?

In this paranoid state, my first reaction would be to announce, "Hey folks! We are on the same boat, and it is sinking." Then they would yell, "Hey dude you are in the wrong building. The Psych ward is across campus."

Thankfully, I am summoned. "Mr. Largent, would you please come to the front desk."

A pleasant older lady escorts me down a hallway, with large-framed photos of nature scenes from the Western United States to a small waiting room for six people of which there is only little ol' me. After a twenty-minute wait, a calm but indifferent nurse tells me, "Dr. Hamlett will be with you soon, he is waiting on someone."

I think, duh! He is waiting on me and I am here.

But in this weak state, her apathy is preferred over perturbed, thus I cheerfully reply, "Okay."

As if I have a choice.

Chalk up my demeanor as being kind to strangers who may someday puncture me. All I want is to get this over with and be home with a cool washcloth over my aching eyes in a dark room.

Fifteen minutes later Nurse Congeniality says the magic words: "The doctor will see you now."

Would love to respond with "I am sorry, but I am waiting on someone." But don't.

Upon entering Dr. Hamlett's private office, a surprise. There stands Dr. Grossman. I almost didn't recognize him since he is wearing a blue tailored sports coat, gray slacks, a crisp white button-down collared shirt and a maroon club tie. Must admit, the big man dresses well.

But why is he here? Is this a tag team match of doctors against my stubbornness not to seek treatment, or is it to give support? My best guess is both.

Dr. Hamlett looks to be in his early forties, which hopefully means he is up on the latest brain conditions and procedures. There are so many diplomas on his wall you could say, "He has more degrees than a thermometer."

Dr. Hamlett graduated from Stanford University School of Medicine. He has a certificate or diploma from Paris-Sorbonne Université. I can't tell what for because it's written in French— which suggests he is either unworldly smart or a heck of a chef.

Thank goodness he is Black. Do you realize in today's world how intelligent a Black man must be to even have a chance at being a brain surgeon? I am duly impressed and thankful.

He stands close to five foot eleven inches, with a receding hairline, intense brown eyes, and a firm handshake disguised with impossibly soft skin.

"Please sit down," he says, motioning Dr. Grossman and me toward two modern steel leather cushioned chairs in front of his chrome and clear glass top desk.

Dr. Hamlett has the floor as it is his floor. "Mr. Largent, as I have relayed to Dr. Grossman"— they glance at each other—

"you have stage four Glioblastoma brain cancer. I am here with Dr. Grossman to answer your questions and to discuss potential treatment." His voice is deep and warm.

My voice is deep with fatigue. "I have been reading on the internet about Glioblastoma cancer and do have a few questions."

He and Dr. Grossman nod as every cancer patient goes to the Internet for knowledge about what they don't want to discover.

"Please, go ahead."

"Let's cut to the chase. Based on my records, how long do I have?"

Not missing a beat, he says, "Every case is different. This type of cancer is difficult to treat. The blood-brain barrier is an issue thus getting drugs into the tumor may be challenging."

"Let's assume I choose not to have treatment."

Dr. Grossman shifts in his chair.

"These types of tumors can cause the brain to swell because of the amount of space they consume. As the brain swells it can lead to headaches, nausea, and vomiting. It's an aggressive, fast-spreading tumor. These tumors are highly cancerous because they can reproduce quickly and are supported by large blood vessels."

"I do recognize the three symptoms," I say quietly, like by saying it louder they would awaken.

"Do you have the headaches when you first wake up?"

"Yes sir, and sometimes during the day and night."

He and Dr. Grossman look at each other like I was a ten-year-old who said his first cuss word at the dinner table.

"Let's say I choose to endure the treatments available. What is the life expectancy, please?"

Not flinching, looking me straight in the eyes, he speaks slowly in a matter-of-fact tone.

"With optimal treatment, the survival rate is usually less than one year. About 2 percent of patients survive three years."

I wonder why would Dr. Grossman take his valuable time and put on a coat and tie to hear such a dark prognosis?

Because he cares.

"Thank you, gentlemen, for taking the time to see me and for giving me the chance to ask some questions. I just have two questions. What will the final days be like?"

"Everyone is different, and you may have some, all, or none of the drowsiness, headaches, poor communications, cognitive and personality changes, seizures, delirium, and focal neurological symptoms." He pauses when seeing my confused look. "Which is paralysis or difficulty using certain parts of the body and the inability or painful swallowing."

"Sounds like one of those all-you-can-eat buffets where the food is not good but you get a lot of it."

They both smile.

Internet research has made it possible for none of this to be a surprise, but now for the nagging question that the internet could not answer.

"Can one of the symptoms of my brain tumor include hearing voices?"

"For that to happen your tumor needs to be close to the Posterior Thalamus scan. It's close but I can't say for sure, without more tests, whether it's progressed that far. Are you hearing voices?"

Not wanting to get into my current relationship with the Devil, I reply, "A couple of times."

Looking like a scientist who may have discovered a new disease he says, "I would be glad to go into this further when you feel like it."

"I will let you know."

Leaving Dr. Grossman to explain to him later that this is Largent speak for, "No thank you."

I slowly stand with assistance of the leather on the chrome arms of the chair, taking Dr. Hamlett's firm hand and again say, "Thank you."

I turn to the man I wish had been my grandfather, take his catcher's mitt big hand, look into his ice-blue eyes knowing it will be the last time I will ever see them, and say, "Thank you for all you have done for me."

Then I leave the room.

Walking back down the hall with the Western nature scenes on the wall, I think, they should replace these with prints of the Dutch painter Hieronymus Bosch, noted for his macabre and frightening depictions of Hell. Inasmuch as Dr. Hamlett, like Bosch, paints a very dark picture.

11

WHY GOD NEEDS THE DEVIL

I arrive home around 3:00 PM, greeted by my four-legged friend who will soon have a trust fund and yet does not care.

After a long nap, it's a good time to meditate. Just 15 minutes in, up pops a question.

"Why does God need the Devil and does the Devil need God?"

Then I hear, "You can't see the light of the stars without an expanse of darkness. How does one know real love without ever feeling unloved? There is no true peace without experiencing anguish. Why get stoned if you can't have cookies?"

"Say what?"

"Wanted to see if you were still meditating."

"No, I am present, but I need a break, so *net*."

"What did you say?"

"Net, calling for taking a break from this ping pong match of a conversation. Let's continue, or not, after I take in the twilight, where troubles of the day can dim with the light."

"We will continue, but don't fool yourself—I don't need light to accent worry."

As if I need a reminder.

It feels good to stand even if it must be executed slowly. The stretching awakens Rhett and we both mosey out through the kitchen and into the backyard. Rhett goes on his rounds checking for new scents and critters.

The stillness of fading light reminds me of when I was 13 years of age and had a paper route. I would awaken before first light, splash cold water on a sleepy face, then peddle my bike to pick up the newspapers to be delivered to sleeping customers' driveways.

On those golden mornings, I was surrounded in silence and warmed by the feeling that all was right with the world. Tension was prevalent in our house, so it was always a relief and a short reprieve to be up and out before the call to arms, known as 'Crazy Mama is awake.' Every pre-dawn I wished my red Schwinn bike had a motor so I could ride far away. The morning ride began with a 20-minute sprint to the drop-off—at a Texaco gas station not yet open—to retrieve the day's papers. It took 30 minutes to roll and tie each paper with a rubber band. Then I was ready to ride, a full canvas bag of newspapers with the paper's name stenciled in black, *The Tennessean*, hung around my neck and balanced on the handlebars. Peddling as hard as my skinny legs would pump, I would fly down the steep hill of our street with the wind upon my face and rifling through my hair. Enjoying the sweet smell of a clean morning, focusing on staying upright and out of sight.

Silence, beautiful silence. I loved being on the bike instead of on my toes, listening for her voice to decipher the mood of the morning. No need for hyper-vigilance now, just the meditative practice of throwing rolled papers onto driveways and hearing the faint thud as they landed on gravel or asphalt. All while being immersed in the coming light. Freedom.

Now, back in the present, sitting in a lawn chair watching Rhett frolic, the wind on my face and light jacket—aptly called a windbreaker—bracing a cool breeze, observing the early spring flowers just starting a new cycle of life. The joy of the simple pleasures of being alive.

I just might miss this thing called life.

BACK AT THE desk, holding a simmering cup of chamomile tea in both hands, embracing its welcomed warmth only to be interrupted by the source of the acceleration of consternation, the Devil. I swear his icy presence has cooled the tea.

"Welcome back, Max."

I sigh and turn on the recorder.

"Now as I was saying, God needs me because She gave all people free will. What good would it serve if you have the freedom to choose but had no choices? Even Disney has villains. My job, my purpose, is to keep you humans in the dark as much as possible so you can't experience the grace of God's light but not make it so dark you give up to that light."

"Do you think God really doesn't understand human nature?"

He replies, "I don't know but I tried to tell her that humans can't handle free will and we haven't spoken since I was kicked out—I mean, left Heaven."

"Do you miss Heaven and God's light?"

"Not as long as human souls are in Heaven."

"You really carry a grudge."

"Do you want to find out?"

"Never mind." Then I add, "Oh Prince of Darkness, explain that 'so dark you give up to the light.'"

"The human psyche cannot take two traumas simultaneously.

It shuts down, gives up, quits fighting," he says. "Dual traumas instill hopelessness that leads to suicide. Here in Hell, we call it 'overkill.' Those traumatized souls who don't kill themselves give up fighting and surrender to God. That's when I lose them.

"Let's say one experiences life's greatest pain; losing a child," the Devil continues. "That's a pain so immense even I want nothing to do with it. The victims of this pain rage at God for taking their beloved child. They blame God for the ultimate injustice. At this point, I have a good shot at bringing those grieving people to my side. But if that same person experiences another trauma at the same time, such as a divorce or serious illness, then that soul gives up the fight, surrenders, quits blaming, and begins to heal by putting everything in God's hands."

"Whoa! Is this an admission? You have a weakness?

He shouts, "No dammit! I have no weakness. I just hate quitters."

"Yeah sure." I snicker. "Don't quit now; finish your thought."

"I was saying I need people fighting, railing against life, making other people miserable. Now some well-meaning souls can make people miserable by prophesying. There is nothing more boring than a born-again sinner. Got plenty of those down here. I tell them, '"If you were such a true believer, you wouldn't have wound up here.' But they're too busy preaching to listen.

"The world needs to understand right now, neither God nor I are puppeteers. We don't pull strings. We just watch how life unfolds for each individual and how that person handles it using their free will."

I need to stand. My mind and bottom are going numb. Maybe they are in the same location?

Standing, and stretching with arms raised, turning from side to side, then I make a halfway attempt to touch my toes. Feeble is as feeble does.

Out of the blue—or is it black—I hear, "Understand Max, the loss of a child—"

"Wait an unholy second, man! I am taking a break. Why do you talk to me when I am not writing or recording?"

"If people wouldn't worry so much, I wouldn't talk so much.

"As I was saying, before you got all excited, the loss of a child or a loved one is neither God's doing, or mine. It's just life. You get to choose how you survive it and get through it— maybe not over it, but at least through it."

"You are starting to sound like a new age guru."

"Shut up, I am on a roll here. Let the readers know that when people commit suicide, there's no guarantee I'll get their souls. Think about it. Those poor souls are in hell on earth. Why would God want them to continue suffering with me? Nor do they end up in purgatory, and by purgatory, I don't mean stalled in rush-hour traffic."

"Are you saying this for my benefit? Is suicide in my immediate future?"

"You have free will. but there is still much for you to learn before leaving planet earth. On the day you were conceived you bought the ticket to a movie of your life, why leave early? Stay around, and see how it ends?

He continues. "Back to the book. The souls who kill themselves can go to Heaven unless they take innocent bystanders with them. You ever notice how leaders of suicide bombers always send someone else to get blown up? It's called career longevity, also known as 'you go first.'

"I have witnessed human and blood sacrifice to appease the gods for thousands of years and the preponderance of victims were children. Yes, I said *victims*. Even I have limits.

There are reports that some crazy-ass people calling themselves

Satanists have killed humans in my name. There have been and are today religious wars that kill people for their beliefs, and some have taken to killing innocent people and themselves to try and enter Heaven.

"When I greet those surprised murderers who have been brain washed—which must have been only a light rinse—to kill, I tell them the chicken and pig story. A chicken and a pig were walking down the sidewalk on a hell of a hot day and the chicken says to the pig, 'Let's make breakfast.' The pig replies, 'Screw that! For you it's a contribution; for me it's a total commitment.'"

"Do they understand?" I asked.

"Of course not. Here in Hell, I bring heat, not illumination. Besides, if they could grasp the obvious, they wouldn't have put on a vest of death to begin with."

I wonder if it's too late to be fitted for one of those in a 42, long?

12

THE 'I LOVE ME WALL'

I come too around 6:00 AM. Rhett is beside the bed wagging his tail knowing that there is food in his immediate future.

Need to shower, shave, and put on my big boy pants. No lounging wear today as I will be looking for loopholes. Not the ones I hope to find in the Bible, but the ones identified within the legal system.

Big surprise. Max Largent has money to leave behind. This goes against my life-long philosophy of enjoying every penny. My will was supposed to read, "Being of sound mind and body, I spent every penny." The main reason to have money to leave is so your children will have a reason to visit you in the nursing home. I have no children and not enough time to be in a nursing home.

Leaving planet earth requires a lot of paperwork, meaning more money for lawyers. There is a Will, Trust account, and Power of Attorney for Billy Bob to send me off into the last sunset without probate.

There will be the necessity to pay for end-of-life care. Just as important is to provide for Rhett after I am gone, so he will have an air-conditioned doghouse and a T-bone steak every day.

THE ESTATE ATTORNEY'S office is in downtown Nashville which is made up of banks, law firms, and the courthouse. That's why I never go downtown unless I am in trouble or need to rob a bank.

Gaylord Edgar Mahomes III Esq. was referred by my banker James White. You want a lawyer referred by someone who sends them clients—or they owe money too.

Lawyers are like doctors. They never want you to think they aren't busy or important, so they make you wait even if they are forced to play video games on their computer. Then with glee, they add their game time to your bill. Judging by his portrait in the lobby it's easy to believe that Gaylord is too old to know what a video game is. He must be sitting in his office counting the liver spots on the back of his hands.

While I am seated, the firm's receptionist, a pleasant young lady with a fetching smile, fiery red hair, green eyes, and unblemished skin as white as new china, offers me "water or coffee?"

I was going to reply, "No thank you, but I will take a shot of Tequila," but she is too young and nice for me to go there. With my condition, there is nothing more futile than flirting. I reply in kind with a smile and a "No, thank you."

It is an unwritten rule that law offices prohibit humor; it's looked down on as representing feelings. Do you get the inkling I don't think much of the legal profession or most of those who practice it? It's called experience.

After 15 minutes of entertaining myself with my warped way of thinking, the young lady directs me down a long corridor to the fourth door on the left.

Finding my way unescorted is an indicator of the size of my so-called estate. If it were for a million dollars or more, the old boy would have greeted me in the reception area and walked me down the hall. If I had several million, he would let me ride him piggyback.

Gaylord Edgar Mahomes III is a rail-thin, tall, and bald old-school lawyer who dresses so Ivy League they must have to water him twice a week. With pride, he shows me into his massive office.

He sits behind his boastful desk that could land a small plane. In front of his landing field are two leather chairs that are lowered so he sits looking down on you. Making it easy to surmise that this is Gaylord the III's favorite view in his everyday life.

I have a distaste for insecure better-than-thou lawyers as much as they detest opinionated self-centered know-it-all clients. I look into his brown eyes shaded by a canopy of bushy gray eyebrows and see a spike of dislike. Good, I am going to enjoy this.

Gaylord's office has the obligatory long leather couch and a round, walnut conference table with four chairs to help justify the size of his ego. Floor-to-ceiling windows on the twentieth floor let in the light of day on his 'I Love Me Wall.'

The wall behind his desk is adorned with a law degree from Vanderbilt. Lawyers' diplomas have where they graduated from but never where they finished in their class. Gaylord also has framed newspaper clippings of his charity affiliations and photos of famous politicians he paid to shake his liver-spotted hand.

Attorney Mahomes appears to be in his mid-sixties thus I am spared the caveman little hand- print drawings on his 'I Love Me Wall' that shout "I love you, Daddy." Self-important men use these works of art to show the world that they must be good fathers while they spend much of their time at the office and the golf course. Their children should write "I Love You Daddy, on the rare occasion your ass is home."

Nice thing about dying soon: I can tell the truth, at least to entertain myself.

The meeting seems to be going okay with my elderly attorney until he says, "Mr. Largent, it is a pleasure to meet you. Is your family the Largent's from South Carolina?"

This is an old Southern country club question to disingenuously make you think you have a connection. I want to reply, "No, we are the Largent's from San Quentin."

Instead, I shake my head no. This gives him the green light to say, "I understand from Jim you require a living will and Power of Attorney. Is that correct?"

I just nod.

With pen in hand, he asks, "Your full name?"

"John Maxwell Largent."

"Who are your beneficiaries?"

"Just one."

"Good, that simplifies things."

Which he doesn't mean since lawyers make money from complications and disagreements.

"And the full legal name of your beneficiary?"

"Rhett."

His condescending grin says, 'This guy is not very bright.' Thinking I might be a little deaf, he speaks louder, "Does Rhett have a last name?"

"Nope. Just Rhett."

Confused, which I must admit I am enjoying, he says, "I don't understand."

"Rhett is my dog."

I can see his privileged life pass before his eyes. Thinking: I went to Vanderbilt Law School, married into one of Nashville's best families—best means they have a boatload of money—I am a member in good standing of the most exclusive country club in Nashville and I am about to write a will where the beneficiary is a dog?

"That's interesting," is all he says. His face is as red as a dusty Alabama dirt road.

I tell him, "Rhett is an interesting dog. Besides, this gives you something to talk about at boring dinner parties."

Still taken aback, all he can say is, "I can have the documents ready in a week."

"Just send them to my home, with your bill, and I will have them notarized and mailed to my Trustee, Mr. Billy Bob Baker, who is not a dog."

I rise, thank him for his time—which I am paying for—shake his hand, and leave a stupefied attorney to his 'I Love Me Wall'.

Then it dawns on me. His 'I Love Me Wall' has neither a picture of a family nor any pets. The poor guy could never understand the compassion for wanting to reward unconditional love.

I exit down the silent hall, smiling and wondering how he will explain to his partners his career has succumbed to creating a Trust for a tail-wagger.

When you can laugh at yourself, you have had a good life. When you can laugh at yourself before others do, you have had a great life.

13

DEMONS

I have been dancing with demons since my teenage years. Only lately have I tried to lead. Since I have the ear of the Demon of all demons—or does he have mine?—now is the time to ask, "What do you call demons?"

"Negative emotions and actions that lead straight to me."

"That sounds like a lot of busy demons."

"The most active are the inner demons in everyone's head, sometimes working 24/7—especially on holidays—when there are no distractions. The spiritual teacher, Ram Dass, once said, 'If you think you are enlightened, go spend a week with your family.'"

"Amen," I say.

"You should know. Let's take your parents."

"Do we have to?"

"Hey, you asked the question about demons." He then throws my previous words back at me like a hard fastball down the middle of the plate. "If you don't like the answer don't ask the question."

Should I remind him that I didn't ask for these questions—or answers?

"Look Satan, if I may call you Satan?"

"Sure, call me anything. It's humans that are sensitive to names."

"Why do you have to bring up my parents? Can't we just let that part of my life go?"

"For the very reason you haven't, which is causing you and others like you to create hell on earth and making my role down here harder to justify. How can I welcome you to Hell when you are already there?"

"Oh great."

"Right-o buck-o. So, let's take your mother. Not to pick on her, but I am an equal opportunity Devil."

With fatigue in my voice. "Please get to the point?"

"Many humans relate their emotional problems (aka demons to relatives), and they are correct. When you swim in the gene pool of life you must understand that it is fed from sources of good and evil. If you can't make that distinction, then you are drowning every day and sinking all the way to Hell."

"Are you saying someone peed in my gene pool?"

"Yes, yours and everyone else's. It isn't as if your mother chose to have her demons or on the day you were born said, 'I am going to take this little innocent spirit and do a real number in his head by passing on all my pain.'

"She was swimming in a gene pool of pain that was fed by a wellspring of negative emotions that were passed down to her from many generations all the way back to Adam and Eve.

"Speaking of the Garden of Eden, here's a question that has always puzzled me. Where did Cain and Abel's wives come from? Who were their wives' parents? Wouldn't they at least be cousins?

With anger, he says, "Ask God, for this is my book. You don't have enough time on earth for me to explain all the dynamics of religious rulebooks. If you took everything literally in sacred text, all professional football players are going to Hell because they work on Sundays while they handle pig's skin. And don't ever again compare my book to the Bible."

I think, don't worry about anyone doing that.

To move on, I ask, "So, our emotional demons are passed on for generations?"

"Yes. Until someone declares, 'Enough. This pain stops with me.' You think you are that brave?"

"No, but even I, the Duke of Denial, has to acknowledge that repeating the same negative behavior is not the way to get off the scary-go-round of misery."

"Max. Max. You know that brings up a scary word."

"What?"

"Change."

"Why is change scary?"

"Change means the unknown, and that is terrifying. I have convinced humans to be more frightened of the unknown than mental anguish. You all want meaning for your pain caused by others, well here it is, some people are just plain mean."

"Question for you Max."

"Before you ask, I left something burning."

"What's burning?"

"My sanity. Let's take a break."

"Not for long, I am on a roll here, and there is a major question for you that's important for the book."

Turning off the recorder, I stand on weak legs, careful to step over a sleeping Rhett and move to a dark kitchen. I take some of the prescribed meds chased by a sip from a bottled water. Note to self: Since you are dying soon you can drink tap water, you know that stuff you were raised on. No pain pills. At this time I just don't feel the need, but be assured when the pain is intense, I will be popping those puppies like they are chocolate kisses from Heaven.

Sitting on a barstool at the kitchen counter I think, Max only you can screw up having cancer. What's that Chinese curse? 'May you live in interesting times.' Here is the Max Largent curse, 'May you die an interesting death.'

This reminds me of what Will Rodgers said: "I want to die like my grandfather, peacefully in his sleep, not screaming like the passengers in his car."

Even those of us walking up the gallows of death enjoy a little diversional humor.

The brown and tan granite countertop feels cool to my palms, so I lay my achy forehead on it, close my eyes, and try to think of nothing, just focusing on shallow breathing, falling asleep.

"Max, sleepy-time is over. I have a question."

"Give me a minute." Groggy, I stumble to the den like a drunken sailor, settle in the desk chair, turn on the recorder, and say "shoot" as in, would somebody please shoot me.

"Max, I have to ask. Has all that guidance you sought on your spiritual quests for understanding and enlightenment led to forgiveness?"

"Still a work in progress."

"I like that. Don't want you forging into forgiveness. Forgiveness is a terrible thing. People start forgiving others for the little things and then before you know it they go off the deep end and start forgiving themselves. Then, much to my chagrin, I have lost them to eternal bliss. There's not a single soul here in Hell that has forgiven themselves. Got a few that have lost their way and forgiven someone else, but not anyone who has so turned to God that they have forgiven themselves."

My, my, he sure is stirred up.

"Let God have them. They must float around Heaven all day singing "Kumbaya" or whatever they do up there."

I have to say it. "Did you forgive them?"

"Shut up, Largent."

Basking in a momentary victory. "I'm taking a break."

"No problem, I am not going anywhere."

"How will I know? By the way, if you abandon me forever, I will forgive you."

"Shut up."

14

BUTTERCUP

Rest does not come easy.

Not helping are these rap sessions with the Devil combined with the uncertainty of when he will appear and whether he is even "real." Whatever happened to counting sheep?

I free Rhett to the great outdoors of the morning light to chase sleepy squirrels he will never catch, but he does so enjoy the chase. Sounds like my love life.

I'm not hungry but eat buttered toast and drink a little coffee.

Rhett's and my home sits on two acres in West Nashville. I love the sound of the crunch of pea gravel that covers the driveway. Since we live on a dead-end street, there are no discernible sounds to compete with the crunch, crunch of leather soles on small stones. Each step announces, "World, I am still here."

Pea gravel describes the size of the small pebbles that cover the driveway. It also describes what Rhett uses it for: Peeing. Each morning he plays Shakespeare. Walking serpentine from point to point, with a quick pace, his brown nose hovering just above the surface. It's like he is saying, "To pee or not to pee, that is the question." He stops, looks around, hikes his right rear leg, to declare, "It is to pee."

The tan and brown loose stones and their sound reminds me of my grandmother Mama Jean's long driveway on her farm. As a young lad of six, I was sent to live with Mama Jean while my mother ventured out to look for work and a new husband, not necessarily in that order.

My sweet grandmother's farm was 90 acres of rolling rocky hills outside of Nashville in an area called Nolensville. There was an aged red barn leaning to one side covered with faded peeling paint. It held an antiquated tractor, old Ford pick-up truck that at one time may have been white, and used farm implements that had seen better days. A few steps away was a chicken house with rusted wire for windows, a pigpen, home to two hogs and a litter of pigs, a small apple orchard, and an outhouse. As she would say, "My home is three bedrooms and a path."

A few years after I left, she did install indoor plumbing. Timing has never been my strong suit.

Pop, my grandfather, died before I came into this world. I bet he died of pneumonia from walking to that far-off outhouse on cold winter mornings. Or trying to eke out a living on land so rocky you couldn't raise an umbrella on it much less crops.

His walking cane always stood by the front door. There were two antique shotguns with walnut stocks hung on round wooden pegs in the hall, like they were waiting for the long-gone soldier to return home and protect us.

Mama Jean would send me up her graveled long driveway to fetch the mail. On those daily marches, I was supported by an honor guard of colorful orange, yellow, and purple wildflowers. Her brown milk cow would raise its horned head to see who was making such noise then go back to its work of chewing grass in slow motion. The sun would light the way and warm my slender shoulders. This Knight's uniform was shorts, sneakers, and a white tee-shirt. My armor was knowing that the Queen, Mama Jean, loved me. No sounds penetrated my young ears other than the birds and the determined marching feet on the gravel.

With a little head held high, I proceeded on my mission to retrieve the mail and bring it safely back to her. Her castle was a simple white clapboard house with its expansive screened-in front porch where she would stand watch for my triumphant return. With a racing heart and small rock in a tight fist, I proceeded on my mission prepared to face any notorious rabbits or chickens that might impede this tee-shirt clad soldier's return. Safely on the front porch from this perilous adventure, I would receive a kiss and a cookie. No Knight has ever been rewarded with such love or needed it more.

AFTER THE STROLL down Mama Jean's sweet memory lane, I find myself sitting at the kitchen table gazing out the window. This spring day scene is of bent green grass and wildflowers that dominate the yard—frost asters, white flowers with orange centers serving as landing pads for bees. Its bloom is said to be named for Michael the Archangel who fought the Devil. I feel his pain.

My favorite flower is the buttercup. Saying the name causes a warm melting sensation on my tongue.

I'm momentarily distracted when Rhett barks out the kitchen screen door at a fleeing squirrel. It's probably some bored squirrel going 'Hey, the big dog is in the house. I'll mess with him and dart through the yard; it will drive him crazy.'

I am surrounded by tall tulip poplar trees and the ubiquitous cedar trees that love shallow rocky soil and cover this property with shade and privacy. The house itself is a one-story brick structure with a small concrete front porch preceded by a short stone footpath. The lack of a view is to die for.

I love this tree-filled yard, the wild flowers, the squirrels, and colorful birds like robins and cardinals. I feel blessed to live in Nashville in late spring. In this setting Rhett and I have the one thing we value most—privacy. If I weren't leasing this house, I would have built a moat.

Owning a house would go against my preferred lifestyle of being a free spirit with a nice wardrobe. My long-gone grandmother Mama Jean would laugh and say, "My Max is just a kite without a string; you never know where that boy will land."

She would add, "I hope he finds some nice girl to love him."

I did, Grandma. I just couldn't bring myself to believe she wouldn't leave me. I could not convey that to sweet Mama Jean because, like most mothers, she carried the unjustified guilt that she was somehow responsible for her daughter's frailties. Through the years I have seen wonderful parents doing all they can for their children only to be disappointed.

This hideout I share with Rhett is simple: Two bedrooms, two and half baths, a wood-paneled den with a fireplace, and bay windows that overlook the wooded lot. The most treasured piece of furniture is a top-of-the-line mattress that has automatic settings where I can adjust the firmness and the position. I do enjoy creature comforts.

Speaking of creatures, here's hoping that dark creature, the Devil, does not put my mental comfort under siege any time soon.

Out of nowhere, I hear, "Dream on!"

THE CHURCH OF LATTER-DAY WHATEVER HAPPENS IS OKAY

After a long-needed repose, there is an uncomfortable presence.

"Thanks for the break," I say.

"No problem," replies the Devil. "I have got till—let me look at the time—yes, that should do. I have till half-past ETERNITY!"

It is about time that he be shown how crazy I can be. Fatigue can facilitate a don't'-give-a-damn attitude. Besides, why should he have all the fun?

Like a child that just discovered a new toy, I proclaim, "There is a movement I am going to start before I check out of this hotel of making memories called life."

"Largent, do you have to? I am really busy with all the BS going on in this crazy world."

With a mischievous grin I say, "Yes. In Hawaii, I am starting the 'The IDC. Next' Movement."

"What is 'IDC. Next'?"

"I Don't Care! It's all about being carefree. What a blissful life it will be. IDC is for me."

"What are you now, a pasty white rapper?" he asks.

"No, but you can wait one minute, dude—since you have till half-past eternity. I am onto something here. Just think, with an I Don't Care lifestyle you are worry-free with a whatever-will-be attitude. I will be cooler than George Clooney walking through a woman's prison with a pocket full of pardons. Let's say a guy comes up to me in a bar and shouts, 'Max Largent, you are a no-good, lying, womanizing coward.' With a smile I will reply, 'You know, you're right, let me buy you a beer! For, I Don't Care.'" Then you think, Next. Is that cool or what?"

"Not to me."

That motivates me to keep on keeping on. "For female members of the IDC Movement, a man breaks her tender heart, and she will say, 'I Don't Care, I have been hurt before and I will be hurt again. Next.' Your boss says, 'You're fired, don't come back.' You reply, 'I Don't Care, never lost a job that didn't lead to a better one. Next.' The secret to IDC is knowing there is always a 'next' with the attitude that it is going to be better and, if it's not, then, 'I Don't Care.'"

"All right, Largent, but what if a crazy dude puts a gun to your head and says, 'I am going to blow your brains out if you don't give me all your money?' Where's your laid-back carefree movement then wise guy?"

"In that case, I DO Care! It's a movement, not a cult. No martyrs in IDC. We don't care, but we're not stupid. I will give him all my money and say, 'If that is not enough pal, I will write you a check. For I don't care about the money.' There are no attachments in IDC. Just pick and choose your I Don't Care, Next moments in life. The more moments you select, the more you connect with your true self of freedom. In IDC, you are free to care about only what you can control, which is nothing but your attitude. The heart of the I Don't Care movement is compassion otherwise it would be for Sociopaths only. Compassion, especially for yourself. Our creed is: 'Inclusive Compassion.'"

"Hey Largent, don't use profanity to get your point across."

"Profanity? I didn't use one curse word."

"You said, 'Compassion'—that's taking the Devil's name in vain."

"Whatever, let me finish."

"If I have to. Are there going to be dues for this IDC movement?"

"I told you, it is not a religion. You don't have to pay to play. Besides, that wouldn't work.

"Why not?"

"When I Don't Care, Next members are billed for dues, they would just say, 'I Don't Care. Next.' When told, 'If you don't pay your dues, you are out of the I Don't Care Movement.' They would say—"

"Let me guess," says the Devil wearily, "I Don't Care?"

"Very good." This is fun, why stop here? "Now, if people do want to make the I Don't Care movement a religion, it will be called The Church of Latter-Day Whatever Happens Is Okay."

"The Latter-Day what?"

"The Church of Latter-Day Whatever Happens Is Okay. Our gospel is 'It is blessed not to be stressed.' One of our Patron Saints will be the actor Woody Harrelson; when asked by fellow actor Matthew McConaughey, who admired Woody's mellow laid-back disposition, 'Woody, what would you do if you had a crisis?' Woody replied, 'I would forget about it.'

"All members of The Church of Latter-Day Whatever Happens Is Okay will wear a little white rubber bracelet with blue letters that reads 'What Would Woody Do?'

That is so cool, it should be on money. On one side of every paper currency will be 'IN GOD WE TRUST', and on the other side will be, 'WHAT WOULD WOODY DO?'

"In our church, we believe you don't have to always be right, and if you're not right, just say, 'Whatever.' It's a new trial way to inner peace. Hey dude, you know better than anyone that the roadblock to inner peace is non-acceptance of situations that cause stress. We are not fighters; we are lovers."

"Sounds like just a bunch of quitters," says the Devil.

"Beg to differ, Minister of Menace, Demon of Darkness, Prince of the Perturbed. Just because someone says, 'Whatever happens is okay,' doesn't mean they should not go about changing and growing. We make changes from a position of strength, on the way to a peaceful, easy feeling. You're not fighting, you're not blaming, you are in the flow of a smooth river of calm heading to a safe harbor. In times of stress, we say, 'No-person or situation has power over me because I am in my Perfect Power.'"

"Sounds like that crazy Buddhist religion."

"Maybe, but with us you don't have to chant, sit on a pillow all day, shave your head or smell incense. You will be able to proclaim, even boast, 'I do not belong to any organized religion. I am a member of The Church of Latter-Day Whatever Happens Is Okay.'

"Just think, you the Devil, have helped me discover my singular purpose in life. I will be known worldwide as Max Largent the founder of the I Don't Care, Next movement and The Church of Latter-Day Whatever Happens Is Okay. On top of a hillside jungle in sunny Hawaii with bright green misty foliage, beautiful tropical flowers, and a warm ocean breeze that softens your skin and your soul, there will be my tombstone. It will say, 'Here lies Max Largent, the founder of the I Don't Care, Next Movement and The Church of Latter-Day Whatever Happens Is Okay, and thousands of my followers will travel from around the world and come to my tiny grave, reverently brush away the fallen flora, lay written messages of love and proclaim to the heavens, 'Max Largent is dead. I Don't Care. Next."

"What the hell, Largent? You take a break and come back stronger than 40 acres of garlic. Can we get back to my book now?"

"Nope, I need to rest."

The Devil replies. "I Don't Care, Next."

16

WHAT IS HELL LIKE?

I am feeling better, as in no nausea and just a little pain. You may have surmised my energy ebbs and flows. Ebbs and Flows sounds like an R&B duo from the 1960s.

It's too soon in the day to worry and too late in life to cry. Why cry now? No one to cry to or with. The closest I could emulate that would be while coming back from the Doctor's office if I pulled over and cried on the shoulder of the road. As my luck would have it, I would have been arrested for obstructing traffic.

"Speak of the Devil."

"What did you say?" he asks.

"I said, speak of the Devil and he will appear. A cliché from long ago, not an original thought."

"Let's move on. What is Hell like?"

"It's a real fun-house." He chuckles. "Screaming, crying, emotional pain, fighting, drama, and name-calling."

"Sounds like an episode of *The Real Housewives of Beverly Hills*," I say.

"Yes, and without Botox."

"Scary."

There are dark clouds hovering out the window. Based on this conversion it is more than symbolic. Rhett scoots under the coffee table, lies there with his head between his front paws signaling there is a mighty storm a-coming.

"Max, think about your greatest fear and then being consumed by it for eternity and that, my boy, is Hell. Everyone has experienced some hell in their life, but in most situations with a glimmer of hope. Drum roll, please. Ta-da! In Hell, there is no hope—ever.

"Here is a parable on how it applies to you. In Hell there is a large table with a bountiful display of delicious food, but everyone is famished and weak because all they have are spoons with exceedingly long handles making it impossible to reach their mouths. The bountiful table in Heaven has the same long spoons but everyone is healthy and happy because while they can't reach their own mouth, they are feeding each other. For you, your table in Hell will not be set with food but with love, but there will be no one to feed you."

This hits too close to home. Hell, it hits like a tornado. Could it be those of us who are trying to capture the love that evaded us as children are drowning? We are busy flailing about trying to keep our emotional head above water looking for someone to save us when we should be focused on how to save ourselves.

Sure, we all do the best we can with the information we have at the time. It's just a shame when new information arrives the lights are on but nobody's home.

"MAX, END OF life can be all about regrets. Regretting you didn't live a significant life. Regretting you didn't take the time given to be at peace with yourself and God. Some folks regret how unenlightened they were in their worship of money, power, status, and what others thought of them. Believing that they were standing on solid ground while sinking in the quicksand of false desires.

"Got to tell you, I have a plethora of rich, powerful, good-looking, smart control freaks, and religious leaders down here who are mighty disappointed. They get here and the first thing I hear them say is, 'What the F—! I had a plan. I was a winner and it led me straight to Hell.'

"You see, stepping on other people is not how to climb the stairway to Heaven. Being selfish in all matters and feeding only yourself, and not others, is the surest way to land on the long road to Hell."

Trying not to sound defensive, and failing, I say, "Don't you agree that a lot of folks that appear emotionally selfish might just be scared and are trying to protect their fragile hearts, and that maybe everyone is worthy of being loved? Just asking for a friend."

He gives off his mean-spirited laugh.

Hoping to convince Satan that some earthlings are lovable comes under 'The Pig Theory; Trying to teach a pig to fly; is not only a waste of time, it pisses off the pig.'

I ask, "Why is it a stairway to Heaven but a long road to Hell?"

With a raised eyebrow, he responds, "One never climbs down the stairway to Heaven, but there are opportunities to turn around on the long road to hell.

"Few ever do turn around on my Highway to Hell because they realize they have to accept responsibility for their choices and—the most frightening thing of all—practice forgiveness."

Boom! The windows shake. Rhett moans in fear as the dark clouds have engulfed the sky, bringing brassy thunder with lightning to accentuate the Devil's dark words. I don't know who his stage manager is, but the dude knows his stuff. I fight off the impulse to moan along with Rhett.

"Max, are you afraid of dying?"

"I admit to going back and forth about the fear of the unknown. Fatigue plays a large part in how we handle worry. Sometimes I'm too tired to care, like now."

"Watching you humans going back and forth with fear in your head is more fun for me than watching bombs being hurled at perceived enemies of God. They might luck out and escape a bomb but never what is in their fearful noggin." He then adds, "I agree that too much fatigue and pain can make you a hero or a coward."

"At this moment I am a scared, tired anti-hero. Call me delusional."

"Okay, you are delusional."

"Let me finish," I say. "Did you invent interrupting someone while they talk?"

"Sure, God listens. I have neither the time nor the inclination to be polite."

"As I was saying before you decided not to be polite—"

He laughs at me, but I'm determined to finish the point.

"I think I still have a shot at going to Heaven," I tell him. "You did say God is forgiving." Now I have a question. "If God is omniscient and knows everything, why do we have to ask for forgiveness?"

"God is not a dictator. God wants you to have what you want but you must ask with your thoughts, actions, and heart. As for me, I want all of you to have what I want when I want it."

He sounds frustrated either by my questions or my lack of enthusiasm for writing his book.

"Finish my book. NOW!"

I reply, "I hear you and I understand."

He immediately fires back, "Don't give me that passive-aggressive, therapist condescending manipulation garbage. I know you hear me, and you better understand."

I am tempted to reply, 'I hear you and I understand' but think better of it.

My, my, who knew the Prince of Darkness was so sensitive? In trying to tamp down his ill-temper, I ask a follow-up question. "You still haven't explained, why does God want us to ask for forgiveness?"

"Humans desire free will to choose their own place and pace in life, right? God has granted that with the caveat that the cost for faulty decisions is accepting responsibility and asking for forgiveness. Can you do that, now?"

"It's a lot easier now that I know death is near."

"Typical human, only offering up responsibility and forgiveness when death's door is about to slam shut on your sorry self.

"Max, what is your greatest fear of dying?"

"Spending eternity with my mother."

"Okay, funny boy, answer the question."

He even sounds like my mother. Maybe they dated.

"My greatest fear is I missed all the signs and opportunities to see the real magic in being alive. I almost died at birth," I remind him as he seems to know everything about me. "I've totaled two cars—thank God I was alone both times. And in my thirties, the Doctors diagnosed me with lymphoma."

By telling him this, guilt has reared its head. That lump on the side of my neck was the first sign of lymphoma. The high white blood cell count was the second. I quickly made a deal with God before the results of the biopsy came in. 'Please let me live and I will be a more forgiving, spiritual person.'

The biopsy came back benign much to the surprise of the

doctors. As they shook their collective heads in wonder I knew why— 'I had made the best deal of my life.'

A deal I didn't live up to. Oh I did attempt to live up to the higher promise—even though it was made under duress—for an inadequate amount of time, but the emotional baggage from my past kept dragging me down. When you have a life-long crutch, you lean on it while hoping to hobble towards the truth.

Here's a little too late self-awareness. What keeps us lame in life is not being able to get out of our own way. Getting out of your own way means stopping the repetitive negative thoughts about yourself.

The thunderstorm and heavy rain have slacked off to the point Rhett is out from under the coffee table and lying by my chair. The Devil's stage manager must be in the union and is taking a break.

Before being distracted by the easing weather tempest, my point was repeating the same negative thoughts day in and night out as a barrier of blackness that shuts out the light to a path of a peaceful mind. We think with clarity when we think with love for ourselves and no attachment to the outcome. Easy to say, but not so easy to execute.

Thinking with love for yourself is a matter of awareness and practice. Thinking with no attachment to the outcome is knowing you are safe. If we desire to 'get out of our own way' then try to like yourself every day and remember whatever happens is okay. You are your own best friend, so act accordingly. Don't say things in that mind of yours that you wouldn't say to your best friend. No one is responsible for your peace of mind, except you.

Where is this fortune cookie insight coming from? Like a lot of preachers and therapists, I can lecture to the high heavens but haven't been able to consistently practice it here on earth.

"Hey, Largent, where did you go? We are on some good stuff—fear, worry, negative thoughts."

I ignore him.

"Max, Max, come back to me here, man. I have a serious question."

"I take all your questions seriously."

"No, you don't."

I keep ignoring him. Tired body and tired mind.

"Max, what do you think will be your last regret?"

I'm thinking about saying, 'You' but instead reply, "I regret that I was not more of a gentleman."

"Well, Max, most of the ladies in your life thought you were a gentleman."

"Maybe, but one can be a gentleman to others but not a gentleman with himself. I have been way too defensive in my knee-jerk response to comments about me or to me. Whom can I blame for that unattractive trait? Hey I know. It's . . . ME.

"The people I admire the most are the ones dealt an unwanted hand in life but never use it to justify anger. I am working to join that club, hopefully, there is enough time to meet the membership requirement. If not, then all I can do is pray that God gives out Es for effort."

"Wait a second, Largent. You are talking about the kind of people I look down on."

"Since you are down in Hell, don't you have to look up to them?"

"Don't mock me, boy!"

I am rambling at the Devil like a homeless wino upset at his imaginary enemies.

That may be too close to the truth for comfort.

The last thing I hear is, "Your Hell, John Maxwell Largent, will be spending eternity not being capable of accepting love."

CAN MAX COME OUT AND PLAY?

Until I leave for Hawaii my travel is limited mostly to inside the house and yard. Not complaining, for too soon it will only be bed and bathroom, with assistance.

With that happy thought, I make a checklist of to-do's before leaving. Rent a place in Hawaii, forward mail, find out what vaccinations Rhett will need to get into Hawaii, send furnishings to consignment, tell landlord *adios* and, the most difficult, tell Miss Anna, my friend and cleaning lady, I am moving far away.

A rapid knocking on the front door sends Rhett into manic barking mode. Opening the door there is a shock, standing there with the midday sun reflecting off his windblown blond hair is Billy Bob Baker holding two archaic brown leather baseball gloves and an old, scuffed baseball.

His silly grin turns into his patent twenty-four-carat smile and with brown eyes gleaming he asks, "Can Max come out and play?"

Stunned by this delightful surprise, I reply, "Come on in my friend, for you the door is always open and the porch light always on."

"I am over the moon to see you buddy, but why are you here and what are you doing with those gloves and ball?"

"I want to play catch with you so I can get to know you better."

My best friend flew all the way from Houston to get to know me better by playing catch. There is only one Billy Bob Baker.

He says, "There is nothing better than two people, face-to-face, throwing a ball back-and-forth talking about whatever comes to mind. Besides, I'm not going to let our last conversation be our last conversation. We must honor our history."

Touched, I smile. "Okay get your ragged ass out in the backyard."

To the backyard we go on this sunny cool day, me in my well-worn jeans, deteriorating gray sweatshirt, white socks, and dirty cross-trainer shoes; Billy Bob is in a blue blazer which he leaves inside on the kitchen table, gray slacks, white button-down collared shirt, and black alligator loafers. Mr. *GQ* and Mr. No Clue.

After giving him a heads up that my stamina is suspect, we put on the gloves. It feels comforting to slip on the old leather glove and feel the history of childhood joy.

In the shade of the backyard, we stand just a few feet away to warm up for longer throws. I ask, "Where did you get these?"

"Like you, as an only child, I spent a lot of time alone and the highlight of my day was when Daddy came home from work. The first thing he did was kiss Mama hello. The second was he came out and pitched a ball with me. That was our time to connect, just me and him."

After a few throws, I feel what he means. Tossing the ball back-and-forth focusing on catching the ball and getting it back to him is like meditation in motion. We talk about whatever comes to mind, our previous adventures, road trips, concerts we attended, people we recall with fondness and laughs. Between catching memories and the ball, there is the comfortable silence between two friends, broken by the sound of a hardball hitting firmly into a worn glove. The popping sound is its own reward. These moments of connectivity between us are real.

Billy Bob likes to say about the wild and wooly days, "I wouldn't take a million dollars for some of the times I have had or give you a quarter to do them again." To me, this surprise stroll down memory lane with my best friend is priceless.

The only moment of awkwardness is when I ask about Diane Miller, my first real love who moved from Nashville to Houston some 22 years ago. I know she and Billy Bob are still friends from when I introduced them all those years ago. But he and I have an unwritten agreement not to go into that minefield, as it left a deep scar in my heart. Looking back—with a little wisdom and a lot of regrets—I realize it was not Diane's heart that caused her to leave me. She even woke me to say goodbye. It was the wall I built around mine.

"So how is Diane?"

"She's fine, although her husband died a couple of years ago in a car wreck."

Feelings are funny things when the news is unfortunate, for I feel a sadness for Diane even though she has shut me out of her life all these years.

"I heard she has a daughter; is that right?"

He nods and changes the subject. "Max, can we sit down? There is another reason I am here."

I am grateful for the break; my shoulder is not holding up, trying to match his velocity.

"Sure. Besides, Rhett is getting tired from running back-and-forth between us hoping one of us will drop the ball for him to fetch." I need to give Rhett bonus treats for using him as an excuse to sit down. I have no shame.

The trees are covered with spring colors, the sounds of birds telling us, winter is gone. I close my eyes focusing on the soothing breeze on my face. Billy Bob likes to say, "If you want to forget your worries, wear shoes that are way too tight."

Billy Bob tosses his childhood baseball over my head. "Rhett, fetch," he calls and waits for Rhett to bring it back to him, which he does, dropping the ball covered in happy dog drool into Billy Bob's glove.

I hold the door for my two best friends, as we adjourn to the kitchen.

Sitting at the small breakfast table, Billy Bob drinks iced tea. I have water and Rhett is creating a hurricane in his water bowl, making it rain onto the kitchen floor.

I offer my surprise guest lunch from a limited menu: Tuna fish sandwich or oatmeal.

He declines—who can blame him—and says, "I can only stay a little while. I'm catching a late afternoon flight."

"When did you arrive?"

"This morning. Like I said, you can't brush me off with just a phone call."

We both laugh.

"Max, there are two things I need to discuss."

"You have the floor, Mr. Baker."

"I have a good friend who is an oncologist at MD Anderson Cancer Hospital in Houston. It is one of the best places in the world for the treatment of cancer and he has agreed as a favor to me to see you."

I smile at his kindness and feel the warmth that one gets when they know someone cares. "Buddy, it warms my heart that you care but I'm too far gone, I might have three months. What's more important to me than having a few more months to live is *Ars moriendi*."

"Max, you've been around too many doctors. You're spouting Latin."

With a laugh, I reply, "It means choosing your own death or to die the good death. Going to Hawaii for my last days while I am physically capable is more meaningful to me than a few extra months."

"Max, are you sure? You want to at least talk to him on the phone?"

"I am happy you came and as appreciative as a giddy schoolgirl on Valente. If it helps ease your mind, I have been to an oncologist at the request of my primary care physician. Frankly, it was a waste of time and talent—my time, their talent. Thank your doctor friend for me but my fate is sealed as tightly as a submarine about to take one last deep dive."

He drops his head and then raises it up and looks at me like he is seeing me for the first time.

To help him understand my need, I say, "Allow me to quote Viktor Frankl. 'Everything can be taken from a person but one thing, the last of the human freedoms, to choose one's attitude in any given set of circumstances.' I have been given this unwanted circumstance and I choose this attitude."

He leans back in his chair and softly says, "Max Largent, still the seeker. As your friend, I will try to understand."

"Billy Bob, as you know that's what friends do, endeavor to understand the weirdness of those they are close to and when they can't they accept them as they are. So, what's the other thing you'd like to discuss with your weird friend here?"

He stares into his glass of iced tea as if the answer can be found at the bottom under the ice. Raising his head, he looks at me with watery eyes that could at any second turn into a fountain of tears. But he keeps his emotions strong while a redness races to his face, he says, "I am in a real dilemma. There is something I should tell you, but I promised someone I wouldn't. I just don't know what to do."

I have never seen Billy Bob so upset. It must be coming from the need to share with me what he feels I should know versus keeping his word.

I have mixed feelings—selfish and curious as to whom he promised and what it's about. Also, I know how much Billy Bob values keeping his word. Breaking his word to tell me would be the equivalent of disappointing his mama and daddy who instilled such values.

After a long silence, I reply, "Billy Bob, let's do something rare for us. This one time let's be practical. Not like the time we thought that it would be great fun to take flying lessons. Remember after the first lesson where we made jokes the entire time and the instructor said, 'Boys, it is best for you, and the world, if you just took up fly fishing.'?"

Billy Bob tilts his head to one side like Rhett does when he doesn't understand me. He looks lost.

I continue, "I know how important it is to you to keep your word and I'll soon be gone, but your word stays with you until it's your time to go. So, keep your word and don't worry about me."

I watch relief wash over his face like misty water over Niagara Falls.

"Buddy, I can't tell you how much it means to me to have you visit."

We rise from the table and Billy Bob gathers his blue blazer, ball, and gloves. Rhett leads the way to the front door. I think of something that I want to do.

"Wait a second, please."

From the front pocket of tattered Levi's, I retrieve a pocket knife. "I want you to have this. I've carried it for years, bought it in Sedona, Arizona at an old wooden General Store with a gravel parking lot and nothing but woods behind it. I remember the wide front porch with two wooden rocking chairs. The store is off Highway 89A going to Flagstaff through Oak Creek Canyon—one of the most beautiful drives in my life. A local artist makes these one-of-a-kind steel-bladed knives with handles shaped out of deer horns. I want you to have this."

Quietly he asks, "Is this from one of your spiritual quests?"

"Yeah, and I've got happy peaceful memories from that journey, so take this as a remembrance of us and our journey."

He stares at the bone-handled knife in the palm of his shaky hand, and the tears fall.

THE WORLD'S GREATEST MISCONCEPTION

"Want to know the world's greatest misconception?" the Devil asks. "My secret weapon?"

"Okay, I'll bite. What is it?"

"Love of money is the root of all evil. The root of all evil is low self-esteem. And when you process that 24-hour-a-day dilemma, you believe your best way out is the acquisition of things and status. The world is full of wealthy wannabes who are so consumed with material riches they have no clue of who they are. These wannabes are everywhere. But they are easy to spot as they always need your attention."

"What if the attention they generate is negative and does not enhance their image?"

"To the needy and greedy, any attention is a reward. They could not care less what you think about them, just that you acknowledge their presence."

"I read that, 'If we knew how little other people thought about us, we would not care how little they thought of us.'"

"That may be true for the well-adjusted but not my guests at the Hell Hotel, where we never close and you can't check out."

"What if Hell Hotel is in your head?"

"Change your way of thinking or die with it. Greedy people make a bigger mess of things than the religious nuts who at least have a sense of purpose. Money-crazed wannabes have such shallow self-esteem, they believe that unless they amass material proof of their stature and wealth, their lives will have been a waste for no one will believe they are significant. Low self-esteem is my secret weapon. The false pursuit of approval is based on a foundation of quicksand that sinks those souls to my level. Even the apostle Paul agrees, he wrote, For the *love* of money is a root of all kinds of *evil*. What leads to the love of money? Inadequate acceptance of self. If one's self-esteem issues are based on control, looks, career, your children's school, possessions, or anything but self-acceptance then I have you in the palm of my hot hands."

I focus on the air moving in the room. There is the sound of Rhett's reassuring snoring, as he lays at my feet. I look through the window for the moon. It is hidden by heavy clouds. Like the moon, I feel covered by heavy clouds.

The wind without design brushes against the trees, moving leaves and limbs in a soft dance. It will be dawn soon, glorious light. A reminder that each day is a new beginning and that I am still here.

Note to self: To have a new beginning every day you must wake up. How to do that? Easy, drink a quart of water every night before going to sleep. Then you will have to wake up every morning.

NOT SURE IF I dozed off. If I did, the Devil doesn't let on.

I hear, "People with low self-worth go through life feeling like they are drowning. Always frantic and frenzied while treading water being pulled under by the weight of who they should be. Life's pool of existence is not deep. Just quit flailing, stand up, and accept yourself.

"And if you can't stand up, then float and not care what others think. Ignore the judgmental, for they judge others because they see in you what they don't like about themselves and don't have the courage to change."

"Put that in the book, Max. I mean it."

"Why do you, the Devil, want to tell the world how to find happiness? Don't you want souls miserable and in the dark?"

He laughs his Devil's laugh, sounding so cold it would bring shivers in an overheated sauna full of sweaty Sumo wrestlers.

"Me, bring happiness? That is scary-funny. Of course not, the book is pointing out the obvious to the oblivious. Hell is my private club and I have the right to be with those that are more like me."

"How do I say this in a delicate way? You are one crazy Mother—"

"Don't go there, Largent. I know you are dealing with a lot and my presence is unsettling, but I strongly advise you to not let your mouth write a check that your mortal soul can't cash."

"I will try not to enhance your state of being ill at ease until the book is finished or you are dead."

"You call that comforting?"

"It's the best I can do. Even saying the word 'comfort' is alien to me. You want to get rid of me? You know what to do."

The clock says it's 4:00 AM. Is it too early to declare victory and say I made it another day?

I realize that the clock is the singular face that hangs on the wall. There are no photos of a wife and children, no images of gatherings with friends and family. I am the epitome of a secluded life by choice.

Brick by reclusive brick, I have built a wall around my heart. The foundation of that protective wall was laid at an early age.

We build a fort around our hearts for protection from pain until it ends up becoming our prison. For those of us with esteem issues, there is no difference between real or perceived rejection; the prison of pain is the same.

This brings a reminder of a poem I wrote after sabotaging another relationship:

Prisoner of Perceived Perception
Please pardon this prisoner
of perceived perception.
Proliferated by parents.
Painful, past.
Passed on to present partner
Preventing the precious, precious
Pleasure of the present
Please, please pardon
This prisoner of perceived perception

My unconscious mantra became, "Please come close but don't climb the wall around my encapsulated heart. Don't you see that sign?" 'Climb at Your Own Risk.'"

Looking back at romantic relationships, their fate was doomed by a false belief each one would end in abandonment and loss.

Don't want pity, I chose this life, and feel hopeful there may be time to understand why.

Some folks have their lives chosen for them by parents, spouses, social expectations, or war. My war has been the one in my head, between peace of mind and doubt. I have been known to call for a ceasefire—as in this moment of reflection.

"Hey, I am still here," shouts the Devil.

How could I not know? His diabolical chill is like a room with a broken window during a blizzard.

"Max, back on self-esteem and lack of, because we are still looking for the answer of why you always felt the need to be liked, loved, or at least tolerated. My work thrives on people who don't like themselves, but humans today are making me sick with too much of a good thing."

I reply, "Like too much Devil's food cake?"

"Stay focused, dammit."

"Are you damning me?"

"No, you do that without my help."

"*Touché'* and may I add, ouch?"

After taking his shot, he reloads: "When you turn on the TV, the news is all about people hurting other people. Even the commercials pander to lack of self-worth. Ever see a beer commercial with obese people? Drink our beer and you will get to hang out with fit and beautiful young people. Just once let's have a beer commercial with the truth, 'Our beer gives you a great excuse to be stupid'."

"You, John Maxwell Largent, sold your soul to be liked. Can you say, 'mommy issues?'"

"I can blame it on mommy issues. I can blame daddy issues too and throw in a 'scarred for life' by a creepy clown at my sixth birthday party. The point being, would you please quit bringing that up? Even Mama Jean in her sweet way during her last days would talk about how her daughter couldn't help herself.

"If I haven't been able to reconcile that with the help of women who loved me, and professionals, I sure in hell am not going to get it from you. My past is dead and buried."

With glee he exalts, "Well, I sure don't love you and you are not paying me. Be perfectly clear about this: Like everyone, your past is buried only as deep as your ability to understand it. While you have scratched the surface of your emotional pain you have not had the courage to dig deeper."

All these metaphors of buried, digging, and scratching the surface are making me feel dirty. I go and take a hot shower. On a stone bench built in the shower, I sit with hot water pouring over my head and upper back. The pain pills have reduced the sting of this self-induced water torture.

The hot water is off. The fog from the steam encompasses the room as I lean against the shower wall and question whether I will have the time, energy, and courage to uncover what I have been afraid to face.

I exit the shower carefully, not wanting to slip or trip over this large brown hunk of a dog standing guard.

Dressed and feeling hydrated from three glasses of healthy tap water, I head to the couch. Even though the Devil says, "You are not paying me," I am going to lie down on the couch like this is a therapist's office. Rhett must want some therapy too as he lies on the couch at my feet.

Laying here I think back about an observation shared about me by an old-time Southern lawyer friend named John Jay Hooker, who is an excellent orator with a wonderful melodious voice. Standing in his daily uniform of a dark blue vested suit with a gold chain which held his daddy's watch, a starched white shirt, maroon club tie. He said, "Maxwell, my boy no greater gift can a man have than a man who loves the sound of his own voice and you, my boy, are the most gifted man I have ever met."

Being glib has been my blessing and my curse.

19

THE SECRET TO ALL RELIGIONS

"Max, make sure to put this in the book."

"As if I have a choice."

"It concerns the secret to all the religions of the world."

This has my attention.

"A young man struggled for three days climbing high onto the Himalayan Mountains through unrelenting cold and treacherous footing seeking a Guru who would give him the secret of all religions. He believed the answer to this query would empower him to become an honored man. After the arduous climb, he found a cave housing the guru of gurus. 'O' wise Guru please tell me the secret of all religions; in the amount of time, I can stand on one leg.'

"The holy man in his white robes was sitting cross-legged by a small fire. He nodded his shaved head and looking straight into the eyes of the young man said, 'Do unto others as you would have them do unto you. Everything else is rhetoric'.

"Lucky for me lots of people don't get this, and better still are the ones who do get it but don't practice it."

"Do you, the Devil, have a golden rule?"

"Sure," he says. "Do unto others before they do unto you. I call it the golden survivor rule. God's rule is based on love of self; mine is based on fear of everybody."

"The most fearful people are not happy unless they are mad. They associate negative emotions with love. As children, their emotionally distant parents only expressed feelings towards them when they were angry. They are programmed to believe that when someone is upset, they must care. These folks never know a stable relationship with family or friends; their life is a never-ending hockey game, because at one time or another everyone is in their penalty box."

"Slow down, I need coffee." I crave an Irish coffee, but experience dictates that flammable alcohol supercharged by caffeine turns craving into raving.

I slip into the kitchen. This kitchen is nothing special as cooking is not my forte. A simple wooden table painted white with three black wooden chairs. On the kitchen counter is—don't tell Rhett—a single man's best friend, the microwave. I considered taking out the stove and putting in a drive-through window for restaurant deliveries. Just couldn't come up with a way to explain it to Mr. Haley, the landlord.

It feels good just to move even if it is cautious. Man, I thought it would be years before I was fearful of falling and not being able to get up, while sober. As Dean Martin said, "You are not drunk if you can lie on the floor without holding on."

Followed in by Rhett, I honor his presence with a bowl of crunchy dog food. Since the diagnosis, Rhett's bowl is always full in case I am rendered immobile. With much gusto, he loudly devours the contents while keeping furious time with his tail. He looks like a conductor stuck in a 4/4 time rhythm. Rhett acts like he has died and gone to Heaven. At least one of us can feel that way.

With a cup of Dunkin' Donuts coffee in hand, I am ready to settle at the desk. I put the cup on a worn leather coaster, push record, and ask a question that came to me in the kitchen. "Are there many souls on earth who love themselves?"

The Devil says, "Are you counting the narcissistic, sociopathic, and psychopathic empty vessels that I love the most?"

"No."

"I say this with a dark disappointed heart. There are many souls on earth that love themselves. It's difficult to find someone who likes themselves all the time, but they have many moments of love for themselves and much to my chagrin they pass that on to others. They have come to realize they are souls with bodies, not the other way around. They have a strong capacity to dare I say, forgive themselves, which in turn allows them to forgive others. That's such a shame.

"Now, Largent, don't tell me you are thinking about forgiveness."

"Don't know if I have the strength for that in this late hour of my life but I am intrigued about why I haven't. If I could forgive myself and others, I would have to start with why I gave away my self-respect just to be liked."

"Max, when you first realized you had been swapping your power for the approval of the fickle, what was your response? Or as therapists say, 'How do you feel about that?'"

"Disappointed and angry."

"My boy, my boy. Deep anger sprinkled with disappointment at yourself, I love it. What's amazing is that you, Largent, still had the capacity to show kindness—which I consider a serious character flaw."

"Sorry to disappoint you there, but I have given you enough to be proud of. Most of us want to be thought of as a good person—"

"Not everyone you know."

"It's human nature to want to be thought of as a good person if it is convenient and being bad is not more fun. As Saint Augustine said, 'God grant me chastity but not just yet.'"

"Have you forgiven yourself?"

"No."

"Good! Couldn't stand you if you did."

"Well, this is one time I don't need to be liked,"

He laughs. "About time. But hold off on that feeling for now. To use a Southern expression, 'Don't want you to get above your raising.' At least not until my book is finished. Then—and this is a big if—if you have the courage and insight to understand yourself and you're able to forgive yourself and others, you will be at peace. But I doubt it."

"Why do you doubt my redemption?"

"Your history," he says. "Like so many, you have been given the answers to questions that bothered you, but you never followed through. All those books you read on forgiveness and peace of mind but never retained the lessons. How about the everyday meditation goals you set and never followed through on and the seminars for inner peace you signed up for but never attended? You have a history of good intentions but somewhere deep inside, you couldn't or wouldn't follow through. That's why I doubt your redemption."

"Hey man, I was going to do all those things but lately I have been extremely busy."

"Don't BS me, Largent. You can't bring yourself to face the truth. You are a scared little boy."

"No argument here," I say. "Since you have my undivided attention, why don't you share with me your special knowledge on practicing self-inflicted pain?"

"Remember, Max Largent, if you don't like the answer, don't ask the question."

"I am asking."

He sighs but continues. "You earthly souls don't change your ways because this mental pain is familiar and the unknown scares the hell *into* you."

"Shouldn't that be 'scares the hell *out* of you?'"

"Nope. This is the hell you carry within you, the crippling fear of the unknown. My job is easy. You decide you want to find Heaven on earth and all I have to do is whisper a warning that you are entering unfamiliar territory. The excuse I love is, 'the Devil I know is better than the Devil I don't.' That's one of my better clichés and tricks; it has worked for centuries."

"Since my time left is shorter than a one-car parade, it is time to face my demons."

"Max, people can't adequately face their demons if they keep blaming others. The truth of the matter is, somewhere along the way, you must carry your own water. Take responsibility."

"Hey man, I spent much time and money in therapy looking for a way not to blame others. Which wasn't so bad since it was all about me. What a concept! You pay someone money week after week so you can talk about yourself and while they sit there and judge you, they can't tell anyone how screwed up you are. All they say is, "How do you feel about that?"

"What else did you try?"

"You know."

"Yes, but the readers don't."

"Okay, okay. There were comparative religious studies, meditation, traditional therapy, hypnotherapy, and breathwork. If anyone suggests the excruciating medieval experience of Rolfing, they are not your friend. I looked for a witch doctor but not even Goggle could find one in Nashville, Tennessee."

"Well, how do you feel about that?" He laughs.

"Shut up, they all had some level of enlightenment, but I couldn't seem to put it together."

"Not to worry, Maybe you will be able to tune it out before you die but I doubt it."

"Like you care."

"I don't." He laughs. "But, like all souls, it's up to you. By the way, I am curious; of all those disciplines, methods, and therapy sessions to find inner peace, which works best for a seeker?"

"That's up to what resonates with them, but Frank Sinatra said, 'Basically, I'm for anything that gets you through the night—be it prayer, tranquilizers or a bottle of Jack Daniels.' In my case, the one that didn't give me a hangover or required a promise to 'do better next time' was prayers.

"Tell me, smart boy, after all our ruminating, have you ascertained why you have the demon of an insatiable need to be liked?"

"To feel safe."

20

THE COLD MYSTERY

"I have heard plenty about your mother," says the Devil, "but you have never mentioned your father."

"I never knew the man; he was a cold mystery. Never married my mother or acknowledged me. Crazy Mama would complain about him then angrily proclaim that I looked, walked, and laughed like him. Emulation without representation.

"Like a scene in a bad soap opera, I was introduced to him when I was 14 years young. He was in the hospital with a heart issue and some of his well-meaning family members thought we should connect before he died. Or maybe they thought it would push him over the edge; families can do that.

"Connecting was not something he ever wanted. Looking back, I feel sorry for the poor bastard. Here he was dealing with a life threatening issue and the biggest mistake of his life, walks through the door.

"Without notice, I was taken out of school by well-meaning relatives for a so-called emergency. I can remember walking down the hospital corridor wondering, 'What am I going to say to this dude?' In his room, his brother and sister were standing behind me preventing a fast exit. Motioning me to 'go on in' like I was a lamb going up a ramp to slaughtered.

"Here is this skinny, pimple-faced kid needing a haircut and there he was, George Bernard Largent, sitting propped up by a mound of pillows like a stuffed Buddha without the grin. It wasn't the tubes coming out of his arm and nose that threw me off; it was like at the age of 14, I was seeing myself dying.

"Standing there not knowing what to say all I could mumble was, 'Hi. I'm Max.'

"I didn't offer to shake his hand since he was handcuffed with tubes and a monitor. He stared at me and after what seemed like forever, he nodded his head to sit down on the bedside chair. 'Shouldn't you be in school?' he asked like he knew anything about me or where I went to school.

"'Not today,' stating the obvious. I gazed at him intently not because we looked so similar but because Mom had told me he had one glass eye due to a childhood accident and in her cutting way she stated, 'You could always tell which eye of George's was glass; it was the one with a glimmer of compassion.'

"We made small talk like two strangers waiting on a bus. I asked, 'How long you going to be here?'

"'Don't know.' Then he asked, 'You play sports?'

"'Yes sir,' I said. 'Baseball and football.'

"'You any good?' he asked.

"'No sir.' That got a grin. Just think, the only smile in your young life from your father is when you admit you can't hit a curveball.

"Searching for something to say he asked, 'How is your mother?'

"That brought up a feeling of guilt, realizing I got caught up in the excitement and rush of seeing him, I never thought about what Mom would say.

"'She is okay.' He nodded like he understood then glared out the door to the hallway shooting daggers at his siblings with his one good eye.

"The unease was so thick you could pave a four-lane highway with it. He offered me fruit from a large basket, but I declined. We both just sat there, him in his Buddha pose and me squirming as Grandma Jean used to say, 'like a wiggle worm in hot ashes.'

"Then the nurse came in to check his monitor and tubes which required me to leave the chair. I took that as an opportunity to end this awkward meeting of a father and his unwanted son.

"'I got to go, and I hope you are well soon.'

"As I reached the door, I heard 'Max.' I turned and he said, while looking out the window and not at me, 'Take care of yourself.'

"I knew that would be the last time I would see him. I didn't tell Crazy Mama I went to see George, just didn't want, or need the inevitable ranting and raving. But, like all mothers that know what we do before we do it, she found out. Two weeks later I was in my room reading and she comes in with a got-you grin and says, 'Well, how was it meeting your father?'

"Frantically, I looked around the small room to find something to crawl under or over to make an escape. Left with no way out physically or verbally the only option was the truth. 'It was okay, nothing much to talk about.'

"Shock of shocks, she smiles and true to her nature she asks, 'Were you able to tell which eye is glass?'

"'Yes ma'am, the left one, where I thought I saw a glint of compassion.' She laughed and left the room.

"George Largent died nine years ago of liver cancer. The night before his funeral his brother called and asked, 'You want to come to the funeral?'

I declined, telling him, "I would only be a distraction but please tell his family I am sorry for their loss."

"I am glad for the long-ago visit. It helped me to realize his lack of caring for me wasn't my fault; there was just nothing emotional there, good, or bad.

"Oh another reason for being glad was after that I didn't have to send out any more Father's Day cards addressed, 'To whom it may concern.'"

21

THE WORST VICE

"Wow, this is cool. You were abandoned by your father before you were born, by your mother at four-years-old, back with her at six, put in foster care at 12, out by 14, and at 16 she told you, you would have to live on your own because she was marrying and moving to another town, and you couldn't go."

"How do you know so much about me?"

"I feed off everyone's soul defeating experiences; that's the kindling wood for my eternal fire. I take people like you with all those abandonment issues and turn you into victims. The easy ones are those who can't let go of their anguish. Gives them a reason in their head to inflict pain even if it's on themselves. That's where I get my users and abusers. Hell, Max, how in the world did you not become a serial killer?"

"I was a serial killer."

"No, you weren't."

"Of relationships."

"For example?"

"It's too late for examples. You should have asked that question when I wasn't terminally ill."

"Oh Max, you of all people should know no one wants to address their deficiencies unless they are dying or crying."

"There is no desire at this moment to relive regrets. Let's give this stroll down memory lane a rest, I don't live in those neighborhoods anymore."

"Yea, sure. Then let's talk about your vices and how the readers can learn from them."

"Not enough time for that either, but I can tell you what I have learned in all these 44 years."

"What is that?" He asked with a lift in his voice.

"The worst vice is advice."

22

ALOHA SPIRIT

After an hour on the internet looking at short-term rentals on the Big Island of Hawaii, the genius here thought, why not call the folks you rented through on the last two visits?

I check the clock—Hawaii is four hours behind central standard time.

Hawaii doesn't have seasonal time changes like the mainland does. They are never concerned about springing forward or falling back when setting clocks. They are on Island time: Always Laid Back.

Being as it is 10:20 AM there, I make a call to Hawaii Paradise Rental Services and talk to Ms. Pattie Freeman, who remembers me. I must have behaved myself on those trips because she is pleased to hear from me. "It's last minute but I'm still hoping you might have a cancellation for a small house," I tell her. On previous visits, I stayed in condos. This time the need is for quiet, privacy, and an extra bedroom for the hospice caregiver. Which I don't tell her.

"I don't have a cancellation," Patty says, "but a new listing came across my desk yesterday and it is wonderful." She sends me the rental's website which contains all the pertinent information, including several sublime pictures to heighten the emotional pull. All show a three-bedroom house of stone and glass that has privacy and 'gorgeous views.' The words 'gorgeous view' is so ubiquitous in describing real estate in Hawaii it is against the law to leave it out.

The monthly rental is more than I would like to pay but as a repeat customer—and agreeing to rent for four months—they're allowing a small discount. Repeat customer. Another form of being addressed I will soon not qualify for.

Look at me with terminal cancer and renting a home for four months in Hawaii. Does that make me an optimistic fatalist? If you are going to die before your lease is up and must leave rental money on the table, it might as well be a table with a gorgeous view.

"I will be there in eight to ten days."

"That will work," she says. "If you happen to arrive sooner, I'll prorate the rent."

Ms. Freeman is a professional who radiates the *Aloha* Spirit. *Aloha* is more than a local salutation of hello and good-bye. The literal meaning is "presence of breath" or "the breath of life." *Aloha* is a way of living and treating each other with love, respect, and kindness with no obligation to be reciprocal.

"Let me know when your flight gets in and I or someone from the office will meet you at the house to give you the keys and a tour. Would you like for us to get anything from the store for your arrival other than our complimentary bottle of wine?"

"No thank you, Patty. But I would enjoy meeting you for lunch the following week to learn how the Big Island has changed since my last visit."

"Lunch will be fun. As you know life on the Island has two speeds: slow and slower. So, few changes, thank goodness."

On my first visit to Hawaii, I called Billy Bob. "Hey Bud, you wouldn't believe how everyone in Hawaii is so nice to me."

He asked, "Why?"

"Everyone appears happy to see me. They are laid back, kind, and I always end up handing them money."

He dryly replied, "Come to Houston and I will be happy to see you, be laid back, and kind—for enough money."

NEXT, I SEND out notices to cancel electrical, water, and cable service at the end of the month. Using Uber I go to the bank, sign and have notarized the forms for Billy Bob to have access to my account, then to the post office to have any mail forwarded to him in Houston. The many obligatory things one must do before moving across town or crossing over to the other side of life.

23

LISTENING TO GOD

Now that I have completed most of the relocating to-do list, a nice late afternoon siesta will be most welcomed.

First, hoping to circumvent being awakened by the Devil, I am going to interrupt him with some questions. Still have on my gray sweatpants and light blue cashmere sweater. The same outfit I wore to the bank and post office. These days there is no stress to impress. Taking off the sneakers, I ease into sprawling out on the couch with a bed pillow for my head and another on my sensitive stomach to hold the recorder. Rhett, upset by not being able to go with me in the Uber, shows his forgiveness by laying on the floor close enough to be petted.

I close my eyes and ask, "Why are people going to listen to what you have to say in this book?"

"Max, they listen to me all day, every day. You people on earth talk to God but listen to me. If you stopped and listened to God, I would be out of a job."

"What about all those that pray every day?" I ask.

"When they pray, they talk to God. When they meditate, God talks to them. You must listen to be talked to. I don't want people listening to God; I want their 'monkey minds' of negative thoughts jumping from mental-limb to mental-limb. Anger of the past, fear of the future—it does not matter to me. Just keep that chatter going 24/7."

"What about meditation?"

"Those that practice meditation leave themselves and their worldly problems with that in-the-moment school of *no* thought crap. They treat their mind as if it is a muscle that needs rest to be stronger. With no thoughts, those misguided souls have cut me and mine out of their lives. When I rarely penetrate their thought process, they have the discipline to immediately return to being centered. Yuck. They know damn well that I work best with the off-centered. They have the audacity while in spiritual meditation to *not* ask God for anything

"By the way, Largent, all prayers are answered; some with yes, some with no. It can feel like an eternity—especially for those who seek satisfaction through material possessions because for them instant gratification is never fast enough."

DUTIFULLY DONATING MOST of my clothes and some of the furniture to Catholic charities. The other furniture, *aka* the good stuff, is going to a consignment shop in West Nashville; I am not altogether altruistic.

The lease here expires in eight months, meaning that I will expire before it does. When I inform the landlord, Mr. Bob Haley, I will be moving to Hawaii, he says, "This is sudden. Sorry to see you go. Did you win the lottery?"

In a low voice, "Not the kind you would brag about."

Those words cause a pause. Bob is a good landlord and person; he respects my privacy and is vigilant with maintenance issues. He is an interesting man. A home builder by trade who has the audacity to look 20 years younger than his age of 70, also owns several rental houses. I once asked. "Why not manage other owners' rental properties since you are staffed for it?"

"I have rentals as an investment and to keep my two sons busy when they are not helping me build houses," he replied. "As for managing real estate for others, I would rather farm."

Now, he pauses before stating, "Sorry to lose you as a tenant, Max, as I hardly hear from you, plus that big dog of yours keeps the lawn well fertilized." He laughs, then turns serious. "I hope this will be a rewarding adventure for you."

I think, yep. Going to one's *reward* is an adventure.

"Thank you, Bob." It's all I can muster to say at this moment.

He says, "I will refund your deposit and any rent payments that may overlap with a new tenant's."

"Please forward any money I may have coming to Mr. Billy Bob Baker." I give him the address.

With a questionable tone, he replies, "Of course." And doesn't ask any more questions.

Like I said: Bob is a good man.

NOW TO FACE the hardest part of parting ways. Miss Ana Lopez has been in my life for nearly five years. She is the cleaning lady, and friend, who thinks she is Mother Superior. When it comes to her subtle hints on diet and drinking, and not-so-subtle commands on picking up my clothes, I rarely adhere to her advice or directions but find pleasure in her caring. She is also a dear friend to Rhett. They started off on guarded footing since Rhett, even as a pup, could be intimidating. They have since bonded. I accuse her of sneaking him leftover food because he acts like an escaped maniac when she arrives and as docile as a hung-over fat man when she leaves.

One issue we could never resolve was her calling me Mr. Max. Since day one of her being on the scene, I have requested, "Please don't call me Mr. Max. That sounds like you are being subservient. Don't give away your power to anyone." She just looks at me with those deep brown eyes and ultra-white smile and says nothing. I gave up and tried to bring some balance to my over-sensitive nature by calling her Miss Ana. She not only likes, but feels she won. And she has. I have never had any luck arguing with women, even the ones I pay.

When she started to gather her things to go home, I say, "Miss Ana, please sit on the sofa; I have something important to tell you."

Sitting across from her with my eyes cast to the floor, like the coward I am, the sad words escape from my heart. "Rhett and I are moving to Hawaii."

Why do I have this crippling fear of a woman's negative emotions?

I look up and see her worried eyes looking straight at me. She says, "I know."

"How in the world did you know I am moving? I just decided this week."

"You are sick, Mr. Max, I have been worried about you for weeks. No food in the house. More medication bottles in the kitchen. You haven't been drinking, and there have been no signs of a lady friend for a long time."

"Miss Ana, you make it sound like I am dead."

She doesn't laugh.

"Yes, I am sick, but I am going away to get better."

She doesn't believe me but is nice enough to not verbalize it.

"Miss Ana, I want your husband Jimmy to have my recliner and big screen TV."

"You're not taking to Hawaii or want to sell?"

"No ma'am, it is too expensive to ship. That recliner has been my favorite resting place for a long time, and I want your husband Jimmy to have it."

"Thank you. He will love it." Still no smile.

"I am going to give you six months' advance payment as a thank you."

"Mr. Max, I don't need you to give me money. I have more work than I can fit in. I work for you because I want to. Have you ever seen me do anything I don't want to?" She is sad and sharp. "Like pick up your clothes?"

"Yes ma'am, like always picking up my clothes." I look at the floor like I am searching for wayward clothes. What I am really doing is avoiding the emotion of eye contact with someone I care about that is sad. "There is one more thing I want you to have, and that is Mama Jean's teapot."

She leans back on the couch. Either because she knows how much it means to me or that this gift says: "I am not coming back."

Mama Jean's most prized possession was her bone china teapot. It is white with blue willow flowers and bluebirds in flight. Its delicate handle, the bottom of the base, and the top are trimmed in gold. When I was a little boy and it was just us living on the farm, she would take out her teapot "All the way from England" and with a far-away look in her eyes and a longing in her smile, she would say, "Max, darling, someday I will go to England and see Buckingham Palace, the changing of the guard, Big Ben, and maybe a glimpse of the Queen." When we had tea from that teapot she would announce, "As a little girl I would dream of traveling to England because there I could be a fairy-tale princess."

There is a sense of sorrow thinking of that little poor-as-dirt country girl seeing herself as a princess, with a moment of hope for a better life.

I loved to hear her talk about London and "my teapot all the way from England," as I was mesmerized by the far-off look of her enchanted face. Even though Mama Jean was living a hard life on a small farm, in those few precious moments she had a dream. Years later when she was dying, she said to me, "Take my china teapot all the way from England and keep it in the family." I have, but now, with no family of my own, I know Mama Jean would want a loving person who has taken care of me to have her teapot, all the way from England. As of today, Miss Ana and one of her daughters will carry on keeping it in the family.

After sweet Mama Jean passed away, I took the teapot home. When putting it high up on the bookcase in a safe place, I looked at the bottom and there, barely legible after all these years, was written 'Made in China.'

Dreams don't care what part of the world or where our desires originate; they just do their best in giving us hope.

Miss Ana cradles the teapot in her lap and with her eyes closed slowly rocks back and forth. She puts the teapot on the side table, stands and walks over, then hugs me like she is trying to take my breath away. And she does. Sobbing into my chest she says, "I love you, Max."

Taken back, I carefully extended my arms so I can look into her sad eyes and say, "I love you too Ana, but it's Mr. Max to you lady."

She smiles through her tears.

24

WORTHY OF
GOD'S GRACE

Rhett is asleep on the cool wooden floor of the den. I gently rest a hand on his furry back and feel his slow rhythmic breathing in its natural cadence. We are connected in this cycle of life.

"What about those souls who feel worthy of God's grace?"

"Lost to me and my work because they are happy with whatever comes their way. They don't blame God or me when bad things happen. You never hear them say, 'Oh God, why have you forsaken me?' They have a knowing that life is no straight line, thus they adjust. They have the temerity to accept their present situation and to minimize their negative emotions by looking for the good in every situation or how they can learn from it. They think of depression as dark weather rolling in and tomorrow all will be sunny. Just a bunch of lost souls to me. No one ever says, 'Oh Devil, why have you forsaken me?'"

"If you forsake me, I promise not to complain."

"Heh, dream on."

"That is exactly what I am going to do."

25

SATAN GET THEE BEHIND ME

I need water but am concerned about waking Rhett. Not to worry; he can go back to sleep quicker than an exhausted bride on her wedding night. While easing over Rhett's snoring body, he opens one eye, looking at me like "Oh, it's you," closes his eye, goes right back to dreamland. In the kitchen I down a tumbler of water. These meds induce a torturous dry tongue. I refill the tumbler before journeying back to the den.

"Hey Max, want to hear an example of how people use me to get what they desire?"

"Alright, I'll bite. Give an example. But please, make it quick."

He sounds excited. "I love this story. A fire and brimstone Southern preacher opened a bill for a $600 dress, and he shouts, 'Woman, you bought a $600 dress! Why would you?' She angelically replies, 'I was walking down the street and I looked into the shop window and there was this beautiful dress and this voice over my shoulder said, 'Sister, that sure would look good on you.' I turned around and it was the Devil. He told me how beautiful I would be in church and how all the other sisters would envy me.'

The agitated preacher, with a volume of voice he saves for the pulpit on Sundays, responded to his wayward wife. 'I cannot believe you did that! How many times have I preached, when you're tempted by the Devil just say, "Satan get thee behind me"?' She proudly asserted, 'I did, I did. When I tried the dress on, it looked so lovely, but I remembered what you said and I blurted out, "Satan get thee behind me."' The puzzled preacher asked, 'And?' With a saintly smile she replied, 'He said I looked lovely back there too.'"

"WHAT ABOUT ATHEISTS? You got to like them, right?"

"Atheists are boring. They don't fight over beliefs or lack of. You never see an atheist go to war with other atheists. They don't say, 'I am going to kill you because you believe in God.' Or blow-up other atheists because 'you *don't* believe in God the way I believe in God.' You ever hear an atheist proselytize about a loving nonentity or see atheists send missionaries to the Vatican?"

"Nope. But I have always questioned dogma. So, are atheists correct in their non-belief of a supreme being?"

"Why not?" he says. "What do you think God does with those millions of souls that never heard of God, Jesus, The Prophet Muhammed, or a television evangelist? Heaven has non-believers and Hell has so-called true believers. It's about how you lived, not how you believed. Those who say you must believe only one way are telling you, 'You can only believe my way.'

"Now don't get me wrong. I don't like atheists because if they don't believe in God, they don't believe in me.

"Here is a *big* secret. There is no right way; there is no wrong way; It's like your metaphor of religion being like a heavy coat on a winter day. 'Wear the one that's comfortable, and feels safe and warming.'"

"Are you saying there's no one true religion?" I ask with puzzlement.

"You are not listening. Any religious belief you possess is true for you. However, any religion that says, 'We are exclusive in God's club and no outsiders need to apply,' needs to get real. Keep thinking and living your way as the only way to God and I have a spot for you right here in Hell."

I share. "As David Foster Wallace put it, 'A religious dogmatists' problem is exactly the same as the story's atheist's—arrogance, blind certainty, a closed-mindedness that's like an imprisonment so complete that the prisoner doesn't even know he's locked up.'"

"I'll say this for you, Largent, if reading could get one to Heaven, then you would be on the nonstop express. But—and a big but—you've got to live the words, not just say them. That entails getting ahead of your past and being open to new information."

"The burden of all seekers," I reply, "is knowing that while seeking, keep believing."

"Max, do you have faith that there is a God?"

"No. I have experience."

26

ON THE WAY TO LA

I'm in transit. Aren't we all? I am terminal. Aren't we all? Let's act accordingly.

 Sitting in business class on an American Airlines flight going from Nashville to Los Angeles, and connecting to Kona, Hawaii the following day. Waiting for the overhead light to tell me I can now lean back, contemplating in wonder how fast time and events have slipped by since the cancer prognostication and the unwelcomed visits from Lucifer. As the plane makes its steep climb to 30,000 feet and reaches a cruising speed of 570 miles-per-hour, I take a final look out of the plane's window at the outline of a city in a valley of green with the brown Cumberland River flowing through it. *Adios*, Nashville, you have seen the last of me, all I am taking are memories, the good ones. Thank you.

 Rhett and I spent our final night in Nashville at the Airport Hyatt Place. There were no feelings of loss when leaving the house for the final time, but Rhett sensed something was amiss as he crawled to the back of the Uber SUV and kept staring out the rear window until what we called home was gone from sight.

 He is now resting in the cargo area of the plane. The airline frowns on tranquilizing dogs for shipment. After conferring with the veterinarian, she gave me a mild sedative to give him before putting him in the crate at the hotel. Don't want your best Bud going on a long journey unarmed.

As for me, so far so good, but stay tuned. Airplane flights are like relationships. You can't help remembering the bad ones, but you keep getting back on board for another bumpy ride, naïvely believing this time will be different.

We are spending the night in LA to rest up for the journey to Kona: a 4-hour 45-minute flight from Nashville to LA, then a 5-hour and 42-minute flight to Kona, Hawaii.

One night in LA is enough for me. It's called the City of Angels, but I never found its soul. The scariest ride in Los Angeles is not at Disneyland or Magic Mountain, it's the Los Angeles freeway system. At drive time it is known as the LA crawlway. When that racetrack does get going, the term is not "start your engines" but "look out!" Four to five lanes of maniac drivers speeding ninety miles an hour side-by-side, switching lanes without looking or, God forbid, signaling. During the first frantic experience driving on this highway of doom, I was, shouting, "These are terrible drivers." Then I realized that to drive this crazy and still be alive, they are Mario Andretti good. Then there are those with a death wish: Motorcyclists. You are panic navigating with a death grip on the steering wheel and your head on a swivel. Then out of nowhere sonic boom tailpipes blare an ear-numbing noise that barrels between you and the adjacent vehicle missing you both by inches, reminding me of what pretty, redhead Genevieve imparted to me about loud tailpipes: "The louder the muffler, the shorter the penis." This overwhelming too-close-for-comfort roaring thunder leaves you with your heart pounding through your chest and your underpants damp. Calling them crazy is too harsh. Let's label these suicidal thrill-seeking motorcyclists what they all aspire to be: organ donors.

Rhett and I spend the night at the LAX Airport Hilton, a ten-minute commute by taxi. Poor Rhett, still in his cage, looks at me like, "Max, I don't know what you are up to, but this better be good or when I get out of this box I am going full-blown Cujo on you."

"Not to worry dude," I tell him. "We are halfway there and tomorrow on to Hawaii, and we both will have more sedatives."

We are scheduled to leave in the morning on a 10:00 AM. flight. This is intentional as I have had the pleasure on previous trips to LA to see all the tourist sites that mattered to me—Sunset Boulevard, Warner Brothers Studios, Paramount Studio, Grauman's Chinese Theater—all from the car. I am a drive-by tourist. Wait a minute. On one visit I did venture into the Griffith Observatory and The Getty Museum, which I am now glad I did.

As this is my last time ever in Los Angeles. I am sure there are several other interesting sites to see but time is not on my side.

On one visit here, I remember Billy Bob called to see how it was going and I surprised him by proudly proclaiming "I have been seeing Kim Basinger."

"You are seeing Kim Basinger?"

"I said, I was seeing her—until she got that damn Restraining Order, and they took my binoculars away."

He dryly replied, "Lucky girl."

27

OH NO, NOT HERE

As soon as we get to the hotel room, I unload a groggy and confused Rhett, grab a plastic doggy bag, and put him on his leash—which he doesn't like. Another thing we have in common. We locate a vacant lot two blocks from the hotel for Rhett's relief.

Back in the room I feed him his dry food and fill his familiar blue plastic water bowl.

Guess who I am in bed with here in Tinsel Town? If you said "a fetching starlet," thank you for the delusional vote of confidence, but the answer is no, unless you think Rhett looks like Lassie.

"Oh Max. Wake up Max and stop all that damn snoring. You know what they say, the louder the snoring the shorter the—."

"Come on, man. I just fell asleep."

"Not true. I let you sleep for hours."

It feels like 20 minutes. "What time is it?"

"It is 2:00 AM. How is my book going?"

I am grumpy. No, make that irritated. "Look, man—if you are a man— I told you I would finish the book in Hawaii."

"No such thing as guaranteed time for you buckaroo. You do look a little peaked; I am worried about you."

Holy moly, the Prince of Darkness is worried about my health.

"Then leave me alone. I need rest before getting on a five-hour flight in the morning."

"My boy, time is undefeated. Time wins every time. It can't be cheated or repeated. Everyone runs out of it. There are no time filling stations in life where you can pull in and command, 'Filler up, I got people to see, places to go and I am late already.'"

28

TRADING PLACES
WITH BRAD PITT

Too exhausted to belabor that I am exhausted, I get out the recorder, writing pad, and pen.

Speaking of tired, Rhett is out cold. Luckily, my fumbling does not stir him. The trip and sedatives have seen to that.

"Oh man, why did you follow me to LA?"

"Follow you? Max, I vacation here. Besides, if the Devil can't be in Hollywood, California where can he be? It is the City of Angels, including us dark ones."

"Hollywood is a cold mistress; she lures thousands here every year with her false promise of fame and fortune only to desert them on the side of life's lonely Highway 101 of heartbreak and disappointment. Makes their sorrowful souls ripe for my easy picking."

"What do you want now, Deacon of Dark Angels?"

"Nice title. I will have to remember that. Speaking of titles, just finish the book. I chose you for you are a great example of a life that deals with fear, anger, and feeling unworthy of being loved. You weak humans need examples to define your lives." He snarls.

Which causes me to realize that this comparison of my life sounds like, 'Oh, woe is me' which is not totally true. For the most part, it has been a good life, compared to many. Now would I like to trade places with Brad Pitt for twenty minutes? Boy howdy!

True, I have issues but this self-centered head has not always been in the sand. Don't need to look far to understand that many people had a much more difficult upbringing. Heck, being from the South I could have been raised by members of the Ku Klux Klan who bought their sheets on the family plan."

I hear. "Or without a sense of humor."

"I need a trainload of that right now."

29

MAKE HIM SAY IT

"What is that saying you people in the south like to use concerning your dirty laundry and life?"

"My Grandmother Jean would say, 'If we all had to hang our dirty laundry in the front yard for everyone to see, we would choose our own every time.'"

"You humans are always reliving the pains of the past. A continuous loop of the same recordings of regrets. Here's the part I love; no one remembers the hurts you caused more than you. Everyone else is too busy thinking about themselves and their own regrets.

"I read somewhere, 'If you knew how seldom people thought of you, you wouldn't care how little they thought *of* you.'"

"Why can't you humans learn to turn the pages?"

"It's easier to talk about it than do it."

"You never have been able to leave the unwanted past behind, even after you wrote a poem about it for a friend as she was going through a divorce."

"I was only trying to help her look past her pain by looking at the good in the relationship and to see the good in it being over. You want to hear it?"

"Are you asking me, the Devil, if I want to hear a poem about finding gratitude when your heart is broken?"

"Okay, ready or not, here it comes."

TURN THE PAGES
When the subconscious of the mind
Looks at loves left behind
Look at them with eyes that are kind
and say:
I am glad you came my way and
I am glad you couldn't
stay.
Turn the page. Turn the page.
Always love until the
Bitter end.
Then smile, for
You will love again and again
Even though you may never get it right
Know that before you go into that long, long night
That you will remember only the loves worth your precious time.
Turn the Page. Turn the Page.

"I loathe that!" he spits. "Even when you are jilted by a lover, be glad the jerk is gone. And even worse, you believe you will do better next time. That poem of yours compounds gratitude with hope. You should be ashamed of yourself.

"You know what. I am going to shut up and shut you out. It's best for your book that I get some rest. In the morning I am taking my last ride into the sunset on a big sliver steed known as Flight 587 to Kona, Hawaii."

Ready or not, Hawaii here I come for one last adventure.

30

NON-STOP TO HAWAII, I HOPE

Oh boy, back in business class but this time on Hawaiian Airlines to the Big Island of Hawaii. When it's your last ride be it a big ole airplane, or a rickshaw, go in comfort. I wonder how many folks would like to say they are going on a one-way to Hawaii?

I'm trying to be positive that my headache will go away before the end of this five-hour flight. It is imperative I go easy on the meds as it is a delicate balancing act not to be overmedicated when arriving at the rental car agency. Not a difficult choice; a head-splitting ache or a head-splitting collision.

I hold a supple brown leather book cover that embraces *The Soul of Rumi* by Coleman Barks. This book contains the mystic's thought-provoking poems about love, spirit, and our dreams.

When the meal is served I ask the flight attendant, "What is this, please?" When told, "It is chicken," I wanted to respond, "This poor chicken died in vain," but refrained from spouting this observation as flight attendants have a difficult enough job. I left the poor uneaten fowl to speak for itself.

Why am I complaining? The folks in coach are trying to

solve their plastic-wrapped mystery food with plastic forks. One of the things you never hear in life: 'Flight attendant, I must have this recipe.'

Even with pain meds, comfort dictates that I recline as far as possible. The airline's slim blanket covers my upper body, their small pillow supports my big head and an eye mask brings about the dark, I try not to think.

A smile appears when remembering Billy Bob saying. "If Max is not thinking about women or money, his mind is wandering."

The wandering mind springs up again with: A ticket in business class is expensive, but why do I need to save money? Come to think of it, the most expensive thing I have ever said was, "Heck, why not?" Later—much to my chagrin—I discover the high cost of "heck" and the painful answer to "why not?" Like buying the Porsche I didn't need or dating that materialistic, man-eating, sexy Shelia who had the reputation of not caring if a man had a past as long as he brought presents. Sexy Shelia was known for never going to bed with a man on their first date unless she had already laid her hot hands on his financial statement.

That unfortunate phrase of "Heck, why not?" never parted my lips when it came to dating married women. I may have been less than wise in matters of the heart, but I was never that stupid—or suicidal.

Speaking of suicide, what's the last thing you hear a redneck say? "Hey, hold my beer and watch this, Heck why not, and have you met my new girlfriend, Shelia?"

MORE SPONTANEOUS THOUGHTS while flying at 36,000 feet, while laying back as the seat will allow, and floating on pain relievers yet daring not to take another pill in fear I would be flying higher than the plane. That would create a new meaning to "Mr. Largent, can you please return to your seat."

I've always admired wealthy people who enjoyed their money. The ones who enjoy giving to others. Can't imagine someone giving millions to a charity and while writing the check saying. 'Heck, why not?'

There are those who need their name on buildings or be recognized for a charitable gift. That is their way of saying, 'Hey watch this.' One doesn't have to be a Bubba to boast.

You ever notice there are no Bubbas in the Bible?

Might be time to cut back on the self-medication.

THE ENERGY ON this flight to Hawaii is almost giddy; there are few business travelers or islanders going home. This is a planeload of jacked-up tourists excited to be going native. I would not be surprised if a few of them are wondering if they had to exchange dollars for coconuts or whatever the currency is in Hawaii. I love my fellow man.

Reminds me of a quote ascribed to Abraham Lincoln: "God must have loved the common man for he made so many of them." That may be true but try going up to a man and calling him "common." Before you do, you might as well announce to those around you, "Hey, watch this."

Among the first tourists to Hawaii were missionaries from New England who came a long, long way on rickety wooden sailing ships, wishing they had airline food. All that way to bring Jesus to the "savages" to save their souls. If you didn't believe as the missionaries did, you were labeled a "savage." The Hawaiians must have thought the missionaries were savages with bad haircuts and dour looks to match their clothes.

The God-fearing men and women of the cloth ended up with a whole lot of the Hawaiians' beachfront property. As the locals say, "The missionaries came to Hawaii to do good, and they did very well."

We are about to land. The nice elderly lady next to me must have slept as well since I forgot she was there. The view out the window is filled with blue Pacific waters spouting white caps as if waving a welcome. I'm looking forward to the clean air and spiritual energy that could survive even savage Christians.

I'm reminded of George Carlin and his jokes about how we use words, like when the flight attendant announces, "If this is your final destination, thank you for flying with us."

Yep, you could say, this is my final destination . . . on Earth. The flight attendant is on a roll. She now says, "Arriving at the terminal," a term that would induce old George to cringe.

You realize this slice of Heaven is unique when the plane's door opens, and you descend the steps onto the tarmac and not into an air-conditioned terminal (that word again!). Walking from the plane to the luggage carousel the warm winds mess up your hair and you don't care. The bright sun and the smell of the salty water says, "Welcome to paradise."

Everything in the Kona airport is outside in God's condition air, including waiting areas, baggage claim, gift shops and security. It was here that I was first blessed with the sight of swaying palm trees, the breathing of clean tropical air and the awareness that this is home.

I stepped aboard the Hertz rental van with two small bags, one with a book by Eckhart Tolle, *Practicing the Power Of Now*, a small book filled with insights on living in the moment. A unique read where you can open it to any page and receive spiritual advice that you may need or want that day. Same with *Time* and *The Art of Living* by Robert Grudin, *The Soul of Rumi*, and, of course, Mama Jean's Bible. Still looking for loopholes.

The most difficult of things to give up in Nashville were a hang-out or two, a few acquaintances, and my books. The majority of the three hundred books collected during the past few years were fiction, but there were many on philosophy and spirituality like Marcus Aurelius and Voltaire. I enjoyed Alan Watts, Thomas Merton, David Foster Wallace, the Zen Master Thich Nhat Hanh, Transcendentalists, The Mystic Rumi—my favorite, of course, Eckhart Tolle.

Didn't pack my tattered, dog-eared copy of *The Tibetan Book of Living And Dying* by Sogyal Rinpoche. Because I hold within me the metaphor of "We are like a glass pitcher where the empty space inside is our soul and the pitcher is our body. When the pitcher breaks and is no more the soul is still here." Maybe not a loophole but a comfort.

I am not a *Tsundoku*, the Japanese slang term for people who buy and hoard books they never intend to read. Truth be told, I didn't read all 300 or so books from cover to cover and couldn't or wouldn't grasp Nietzsche or Franz Kafka. I am not an intellectual, and feel fortunate to spell it, but enjoy the seeking, learning, and insight of interesting writers who lead interesting lives. There is no reason to bring more books without knowing how long I will be able to read.

The only photo, packed for this final journey, is an old black and white snapshot of Mama Jean's little farmhouse with her standing on the wide front porch, summer sun with her lovely, weathered face, open right hand shading her hazel eyes like she is looking far into the future. I like to think she could see I would take her all the way to Hawaii, in my heart.

I didn't bring many articles of clothing as there is no dress code on the Big Island neither is there one at the crematorium, well, at least for me there isn't.

Of all places, waiting here in the Hertz lobby to be assigned a vehicle, the immediacy of being a short-timer is becoming overwhelming. I have been so busy moving, selling stuff, planning the trip, sending legal documents to Billy Bob, arranging for Doctor Grossman to set me up with North Hawaii Hospice, and renting a house that I haven't focused on "This is it; no turning back." It hits me like an emotional train wreck. The punch in the gut of recognizing there are people and places I will never see again. Such as this is the last time in an airport. Is it a blessing to be aware of our last of anything, or is it a curse? Only time—or lack of—will tell.

Of all the visits made to this Hertz rental counter in Kona, this one is intense with awareness. Like being aware that I am *not* going to be the one to turn in the car. What was once the mundane experience of traveling is now an adventure in and of itself. I notice the beauty of the top of the palm trees swaying doing their own hula dance for all to see and the blue cloudless sky providing the perfect backdrop. Then an impact: I notice a frail white-haired lady being lovingly assisted by what must be her grandchildren. This jolt of loss is overwhelming, a reminder of not knowing a family's love before passing on.

Stop it, I tell myself. Let it go. Besides, it must be in the fine print of the rental agreement that "there is no crying at the Hertz counter" in heavenly Kona Hawaii. Need not dwell on the last of anything; just live in the moment. Be that as it may, it is still discombobulating to know tomorrow belongs to others.

They assign me a white Nissan SUV Rogue. What a world! Japan bombs Pearl Harbor and now we are renting their cars in Hawaii. When I phoned the Hertz call center to reserve a vehicle in Kona, the pleasant lady that must be reading from a form, asked. "Do you plan on driving out of state?" While trying to figure out how one drives out of the state in Hawaii, I replied, "Not very far." As she was contemplating what that meant, I rebounded with an even tone of, "No, I don't plan to drive out of state, but if I do you will be the first to know."

Another good component about knowing you are not long for this world is that you have no compunction to correct people. I never corrected myself, so what gives me the right to correct others?

3 1

HOME

It's a short drive to the Animal Quarantine Station. Hawaii has no history of rabies and intends to keep it that way. For Rhett to have a direct release at the airport and not spend up to 30 days in quarantine entailed hiring a local veterinarian service to make sure all the paperwork was in order upon our arrival. Before we started this journey, the Nashville vet had to inject Rhett with a microchip listing his rabies and booster shots. The fees and all the paperwork for direct release were more than worth it for Rhett's emotional state and mine.

Upon arrival, I'm told, "He'll be out in about 15 minutes." I took that time to watch airplanes take off and land with the sun gleaming off their wings.

There he is! My furry friend appears happy to see me but while his tail is wagging, he is staring at me like the town drunk trying to figure out 'why are there three of him and is he the one in the middle?' This reminds me of whenever a girlfriend wanted to talk about my difficult childhood. It would go like this: with a downcast head I'd tell her, "My grandfather was the town drunk." She'd say, "How sad that is . . ." I'd reply, "Yes, especially since he lived in Chicago."

And, I wonder why I am alone.

I thank the Kona Veterinarian Service representative, with a name tag that says 'Jane Gay', a young woman with a sweet disposition and engaging smile. What a good life she has living in paradise and working with animals that she obviously loves. How do I know she loves animals? Because Rhett is rubbing up against her leg like he never wants her to leave. She could be the answer to my main worry, who will take care of Rhett when I am gone?

"Rhett seems smitten with you."

She smiles. "I am with him; he is a sweetie."

Make a mental note to pass her name and workplace info on to Billy Bob.

Taking his leash we walk to a graveled space by the parking lot so he can pee like a racehorse. Then he receives the always appreciated treat.

So thankful Rhett is glad to see me, or maybe it's the water and treats. Got to love dogs. Life is simple. "Pee, treat, put me in the front seat, when do we eat?"

3 2

ON THE QUEEN'S HIGHWAY

Turning left onto Queen Ka'ahumanu Highway, my sidekick Rhett 'the Wonder Dog' as in, "I wonder how I got here?", sticks his big head out the window, encouraging the Hawaiian trade winds to blow his brown and black hair around his perked-up ears.

His inquisitive brown eyes for the first time take in mountains which are to the right and way off to the left his first glimpse of the massive blue Pacific. The mountain-side has a long gradient approach to the ocean mostly covered with volcanic black lava rock. The lava rock edges to the highway then picks up again on the other side to flow into lush green patches of grass and tall swaying palm trees.

Spaced out along the coastline are multi story hotels and condos with beautiful man-made landscaping that God would have created. As Dorothy Parker would say, "If he had the money." The Big Island of Hawaii has more land than Texas and, at one time, had the bragging rights as the largest cattle ranch in the world. Parker Ranch, once 250,000 acres. It predates all the Texas ranches by 30 years.

The Big Island is one of the most ecologically diverse places in the world where you will find eight of the world's 13 sub-climate zones such as desert tropical, subtropical monsoon, temperate, and tundra.

When identifying the unique nature on the Big Island you have to include five of the world's volcanoes: Mauna Loa and Hualalai are considered active as they may erupt in 1,000 years or less. Mauna Kea and Kohala are extinct. Then there is the famous Kilauea on the southern part of the Big Island. When Kilauea happens to erupt, it is an amazing sight, especially at night. A slow creeping stream of fire, smoke and molten lava falling into the ocean causing the island to enlarge. Because of Kilauea the Island has grown around 500 acres since 1994. Hawaii is the ever-growing state. To the Hawaiians, Kilauea is known as the deity Pele, who creates new land, destroys the old and must be respected.

There should be a *big* sign where the flaming lava flows down from the mountain creating the growing shoreline, that says, "Hawaii. We never know completion."

Pele can sometimes belch, burp, and spew sulfur, mercury, and other chemicals into the atmosphere, which can induce difficult breathing, eye burning and coughing. Not to mention some amazing sunsets. The locals who don't fear Pele's wrath call it, "The hole in God's muffler."

DURING THE WINTER on the Big Island of Hawaii you could ski down the mountain of Mauna Kea, then ride your horse over ranch land to the beach and go surfing. Gnarly, dude!

One last tidbit about Mauna Kea, if measured from its base at the bottom of the ocean it would be the tallest mountain in the world.

With most days of clean air, beautiful beaches, and spiritual energy the Big Island is laid back and calm. Reminding me of what my buddy Larry Lewis, who was in charge of the kitchen at California Men's Colony Prison, would say about the inmates he supervised, "Try telling a man serving two life sentences to hurry up."

Hawaiians are lucky to be serving two life sentences—world time and Island time.

Easing behind a slow-moving, mud-splattered, gray dinged-up old Ford pickup, I notice a faded bumper sticker that says it all, "Slow down. You are not on the mainland."

This peaceful spiritual energy may be why some people choose to make Hawaii their launch pad for the final journey. Folks like Joseph Campbell, who taught comparative religion and wrote *The Hero with a Thousand Faces*—that was the inspiration for the movie *Star Wars*—and the world-famous pilot Charles Lindbergh made Hawaii their final resting place.

When Charles Lindbergh was told that if he treated his cancer in a New York City hospital he might live 6 months longer, he is said to have replied, "I would rather live one day on Maui than one month in New York."

I can relate.

33

OUR ESSENCE

Cruising on this blacktop highway like a surfer riding the perfect wave, just going with the flow and happy to be here. While gazing on the horizon my mind starts to wander.

Eckhart Tolle was asked by a grieving mother, "I lost my six-year-old son two years ago and I grieve every day, what can I do?"

Tolle asked in return, "Did you love your child's essence?"

"Of course."

"Well, his essence never leaves you. It is always with you and always will be."

Here's to my essence being available to the few friends and lovers that had the interest and curiosity to look deeper and to gaze upon the shooting star known as our time together. I hope they will smile.

A grin and warmth appear when a thought says, "Maybe one of the past loves, when alone in her nursing home, will think of me and I will be her last giggle."

May your essence be in the hearts of many for a long, long time.

3 4

MIRACLE

Lifting my left hand out the window to feel the current of tender sea air slip through welcoming fingers, I recall reading, 'The odds of being born are one in four hundred quadrillion.'

So, if someone says to you, 'I wouldn't go out with you in a million years', think positive and be glad they didn't say 'never in four hundred quadrillion years.'

Everyone born is the winner in the race called life. No matter how short, long, or difficult the run.

Here and now it's all gratitude for living 44 years in interesting times, with phones that take pictures, Viagra, and one-thousand-thread count Egyptian cotton sheets delivered to your home the next business day, and the people I have known.

This comes under 'the last bite of the cookie theory,'. Ever notice how we chop away at a sweet cookie then realize, whoa, there is only one bite left. Causing an immediate pause, allowing the sweetness to sit on your tongue, savoring the flavor. I am taking the last bite of this cookie called life

Gliding along with a relaxed foot on the accelerator, listening to soothing Hawaiian music from radio station KMXX 101.5 FM, it is a glorious moment.

THE QUEENS HIGHWAY ends at Akoni Pule, also called Highway 270, where we take a left turn to Kawaihae. A natural harbor that the U.S. Corps of Engineers dredged in the 1950s, allowing barges and small ships to enter. Kawaihae is also where the American missionaries landed in 1820 and for what they did to the Hawaiians it may be where the term "missionary position" was first coined. I can't recall seeing a roadside monument making that declaration but will keep looking.

The great King Kamehameha I reigned here. He is called great because he united all the Hawaiian Islands in 1810. I wouldn't say he was a bad dude, but his rival chiefs ended up like a few of Henry VIII's wives.

This small corner of the Island is known as Kawihe. Here, if you are lucky, you will discover Spencer Beach Park. A delightful find as it is less congested than the tourist beaches. Along the road are a few local restaurants, a convenience store with gas, and a couple of gift shops. Gift shops are Hawaiian for, "We can no longer behead you, but we will surgically remove you from your wallet."

3 5

KOHALA BY THE SEA

We veered right to stay on Highway 270. A few yards later make a left turn to stop at the Ohana Fuels convenience store for a few essentials, mostly just dry dog food, coffee, bread, Wheaties, and tuna in a can.

Back in the Rogue and up the hill for 20 minutes we enter Kohala by the Sea—a hillside gated development of new homes with palm tree-laden lots, all with a panoramic view of the ocean. The rental house is a third of the way up the hill on the right with no immediate neighbors. I am rewarded with the opulence of an unencumbered view of the sometimes blue but always majestic Pacific.

I am here for the atmosphere.

Even with the joy of arriving at our destination, I am tired and take time unpacking the car. These days consist of two speeds: slow and stop. Need to stop and catch a breather and watch Rhett race around the yard discovering new scents. He likes it here.

Rhett's blue bowl is now filled with dog food that he devours, showing no side effects from the long plane ride.

Could not have asked for a more perfect place to be at peace.

Did I hear a dark laugh?

As we enter the front door, we are greeted by a glass wall in the living room that faces a flat green lawn bordered by a two-foot-high man-made boundary wall of black and brown lava rock. In the far distance the aqua blue lazy ocean waves are soothing each other. This calmness is facilitated by mild winds.

THE HOUSE HAS Brazilian wood floors, a vaulted ten-foot ceiling of blonde wood. The living room and dining area are combined with an open kitchen. The two guest bedrooms and the master bedroom are on opposite sides of the house.

I step from the living room onto a gray concrete lanai with two wooden lounge chairs with dark blue cushions, a wooden dining table capable of seating four, and a daybed hutch built into the side of the house. Inside, I could not care less about the kitchen as food these days is more about sustenance than taste. The master bedroom has floor-to-ceiling glass doors, two that open to the mountains of Mauna Kea, Mauna Loa, Hualalai, and Kohala, and two that allow the luxury of an unlimited view of forever, which is said to be a long way.

Petting Rhett's appreciative head he hears, "My boy, we are home." He wags his tail in agreement.

I leave the suitcase and duffel bag opened but unpacked; tomorrow is another day, Scarlett. Opening the four glass doors to the immediate world, I lie across the bed and drift into a sound sleep while saying a prayer that the Devil will not wake me. All I am asking for at this moment is, "Please let me rest before the Devil puts me back to the test, Amen."

IT IS DARK when I awake. Wow! I slept six hours. Rhett is at the foot of the bed and awake.

Tonight is the first night of my last days on earth and what a glorious night it is, illuminated by a full moon. There are no clouds to dim its glow, and present are stars as accents to enhance its power. A night so still it could make an owl sleep.

Then I remember the dream.

36

PERMANENT IMPERMANENCE

The Devil asks, "Guess what my two favorite words are?"

"Okay, I'll bite. Reel me in."

"They are 'me' and 'mine', heard in kindergartens and courtrooms. When people say, 'That's mine,' what they are saying is, 'That is me.'

The first word a child learns is 'mine.' Even God agrees with me and chuckles when she hears 'mine' over and over from the same souls. 'My soul, my life, my spouse, my car, my career.' You humans don't own anything and yet you are always identifying with impermanence. Everyone is permanently in impermanence.

"Your life and all your possessions are on loan. It's up to everyone how they treat—or mistreat—their short-lived life. By the way, not a very good job with the environment and endangered species, such as yourselves.

"I love it when I hear, 'that's mine,' because you are identifying with objects and things—not with God. I titillate you with titles and toys, diverting your attention away from Spirit and toward me."

"Any chance of you titillating me by going away?'

Ignoring this, he goes on. "One of my saddest days as the Devil came when this nun in a nunnery—"

"Where else would she be?" I ask.

"Let me tell the story. It's maddening. Sister Mary Margaret, who was loved by all the other nuns, had one possession, a beautiful water pitcher that had been in her family for generations. One day a novice nun was cleaning Sister Mary Margaret's room and, by accident, she knocked the beautiful pitcher to the stone floor destroying it. Over the top distraught, the novice nun ran crying to Sister Mary Margaret saying, 'O Sister please forgive me, I have shattered your water pitcher, your prized possession.' And do you know what that misguided Sister Mary Margaret had the nerve to say? 'O, thank God; I now have nothing to be attached to.'

"By believing she owned something, I had at least a glimmer of hope to divert her attention. With her having nothing to identify with but God, she was lost to me forever. A tragedy."

"Only to you."

37

WHAT HAVE I DONE?

It's been four days since we landed, entailing nothing but sleep and getting up for the bare necessities like meds, sometimes eating, and always making sure Rhett has plenty of food and water. I even left the bedroom doors propped open for him to exit at his leisure.

Starting to sound like the optimist in a nursing home, "Hey, I can sit up, eat solid foods and still squeeze the ball."

Rhett lays his lovable body on the sealed concrete deck as I recline on a blue cushion supported by the wooden ship of a lounge chair. Both of us are still and witnessing the glorious night and feeling a warm delicate breeze. The moon is high, surrounded by luminous stars; it feels possible to touch the moon by reaching just a little higher. Giving false hope I might be able to squeeze that ball.

In this stillness and light I relax, until abruptly my mind wanders to, 'What have I done?'

I left everyone I've ever known, good and bad. Abandoned all accumulated material possessions along with their reminders of good times. No more familiar streets with shortcuts, no more places where someone knew my name, all to come here as a stranger. All this effort and expense for the uncertainty to die in calmness and beauty. It would have been simpler to step in front of a speeding beer truck. But why try to simplify a complicated life and frustrate a bunch of good ol' boys and girls waiting on their beer?

I admit to relishing the uniqueness of marching to the beat of a different drum. I once shared that cliché about myself to Billy Bob, and he replied, "True, Max. You have always marched to the beat of a different drum, but what if that beat never changes?"

There was no answer then and I still have no answer now.

This reactive spur-of-the-moment parade feels like it is led by a drum major of doom. He is marching me way too fast down a dead-end street of no return. Who am I kidding? The Devil didn't lead me here; this is my doing.

When you reach the point where you realize you're the leader of the march down life's dead end, it brings awareness too, I am going to be the first one to hit the wall.

One minute I am driving to the doctor's office in Nashville and the next I am in Hawaii looking for directions to the Crematorium on Hulikoa Drive.

Too late now Buck-O. You are here. Too bad, so sad. You said this is what you wanted, now you got it. There is no going back.

What am I scared of? Facing the end alone? Nah, I don't fear death, much.

Loneliness is my friend. If I just wanted to die alone, I could have invited all honest politicians to join me in my final hours.

It doesn't have to be life-and-death decisions that give rise to doubt. I have had more than my share of doubt. Who hasn't? Then it dawns on me: I have never been alone because my constant companion doubt has always been in my head doubting the true intentions of others, and myself.

While looking into this dark night of my soul, there is the knowing I never doubted God. Yes, there were moments in the emotional pain of youth when I blamed God for an inconvenient sense of humor, aptly called my upbringing. There is a country song title if I ever heard one— "My Upbringing Was My Downfall." Blaming God is just a good way to avoid the truth. God and I did reach an understanding when somewhere around age 15, that I wouldn't blame her for my so-called childhood, and she wouldn't blame me for the propensity for profanity that might slip and include her name.

Even what is said to be one of the happiest days of your life can bring doubt. Take the bride dressed in white looking like the topping on the world's tallest meringue pie. She shuffles down the aisle, like she has to stop and count each step before taking another, with a church full of eyes watching her, and up ahead she sees the handsome nervous man she is going to marry. Wearing the obligatory universal sweet bride smile it dawns on her, *Let me get this right. I am agreeing to having sex with only this guy for the rest of my life for a ring?*

Doubt doesn't care who you are. That is why you see fathers walking their daughters down the aisle arm-in-arm: He is *not* giving the bride away; he is keeping her from running away.

The father, who doesn't care for his new son-in-law to be, is thinking, *I could have bought a big boat for what this circus is costing and you, young lady, are going to perform.*

Am I scared of the unknown?

Everybody dies. I've never heard of anyone dying and then reappearing to say, "I am back, I didn't like it."

What is this? Fatigue? You wanted to die in paradise. Well, dude, you are here and *now* you ask for it all to rhyme in a poetry of reason.

Yet here I am, lying in a lounge chair under a brilliant full moon in Hawaii with my best friend next to me, feeling the salt air on my skin and the calm of the night.

Picking up the ever-present pen and pad, I compose a *haiku* poem:

Will I die
without doubt?
I doubt it.

38

SURRENDER

Soon there will be the requirement of assistance for such outings, but today I can drive and shop—just not too far or for too long a time.

I love being in this house and keeping the windows and doors open for cross ventilation. The warm salty air is welcomed and a continuous reminder to breathe deep, while I can.

Rhett appears settled and comfortable. He never leaves my side, except for his visits to the yard for relief and looking for tree squirrels to chase.

Don't have the heart to tell him the only squirrels in Hawaii are tackily dressed tourists trying to look native while acting nuts. So many people travel so far from home to be their true selves. Look who's talking.

The food run is uneventful and quick. I can't recall ever going to the store for both of us and coming back with more food for Rhett than for me. This lack of appetite is not all bad; I save money and my clothes are so loose they could be called promiscuous.

It's late afternoon and we move to the lanai where I bring a pillow from the bed to hold over my shrinking belly. The pillow is comforting and instills a sense of security as I hug it with closed eyes and allow the trade winds to encompass me like a cotton baby blanket.

It is dark when I wake. Can't believe Rhett let me sleep that long, but I'm grateful for his indulgence.

Lying here with questions clinging to me like a bad habit. I rise from the comfort of the cushion, plant both feet on the cool deck, step onto the dew-covered grass, and walk in the direction of the moon and the ocean. Rhett rustles awake and walks with me.

I stand on the lawn, the grass peeking between my toes. The light from the house fades behind me leaving exposure to the night. I breathe air so clean it lightens my heart. The flat moon's reflection jumps off the Pacific, up the cliffs, across the highway, and up this hill and touches me.

Floating in a moon bath, the full moon's vivid light surrounds me. Standing here in gray cotton lounge pants, tee-shirt, and bare feet, I am illuminated in a peacefulness I have never known. I raise my arms as high and wide as they can unfold. I reach above my head and lean my head back. From somewhere deep inside of myself, from a place that I don't recognize I feel a connection—could it be this inner-pilgrim has blindly found his way home?

With words never spoken before, I address God. "I surrender God. I surrender to you. Tell me what you would have me do. I fight no more. I am not in control. I have never been."

Falling to my knees on earth that was created millions of years ago by the spiritual entity I am imploring to, I clutch my chest and cry and repeat, "I am not in control."

Tears from the past well up. I cry over the pain of my parents, the pain of people who've hurt me, and for the people whom I have hurt. I beg forgiveness. I give forgiveness. My head and shoulders shudder. My entire body convulses back and forth with surging energy. Then I am covered in an invisible shroud of serenity. I am free.

I am aware of the dampness of the ground and the clean smell of grass.

The release of so much energy at once has left me weak. With caution, I rise and touch a concerned Rhett. He stands, nuzzling my leg with his head letting me know he is here for me. Then he leads the way, turning a head with concerned eyes every few steps to check that I am still with him. After floating across the lawn to the lanai, it becomes necessary to lean on the lounge chair for support.

I stumble on weak legs through the living room, making it to the corner of the dining room table. It's hard, wooden surface says. "Got you." Just need a few more steps to reach the bed. Rhett, still by my side, watches every feeble attempt to slide one leg in front of the other. I make it to the bed and fall face first, leaving a deep impression on the pillow.

I long for sleep and pray for strength.

Mark Twain wrote: "The two most important days of your life are the day you are born, and the day you realize why."

I am still searching for the why, but I may be close.

The last thing I hear.

"There is more to come." Then the laugh.

GOING TO HOSPICE

It's been ten days of solitude, writing, rest and reflection. I have not been looking for female companionship. What good would it do? I would be like the dog always chasing a bus and once he caught it, he would go "Uh-oh, what do I do now?"

Could lead to a unique pickup line, "Hi, would you like to go out with me? I am going to die soon and if you are nice, I will put you in my will."

Sleep was my friend last night. It came early and stayed late, aided by all four doors of the bedroom being propped open, the two parallel with the mountain view and the two facing the ocean. Lying here, thriving on heaven's breath of healing brought by a cool breeze flowing across the room.

Grateful for the gift of sleeping for nine and half hours. I am resigned that slumber is a gift, sometimes given early but usually arriving late. Feeling tired, however, nothing that two cups of strong Kona coffee can't cure.

Just feed my best buddy his can of real meat—real as in its horse meat—and I almost finish one biscuit of Shredded Wheat with milk. Food doesn't have the hold that it used to. Dr. Grossman did say, "Loss of appetite is common among cancer patients."

Thankfully that doesn't apply to Rhett. I sometimes remind him that his food would taste better if he chewed it.

After our breakfast, it's time to take the 25-minute drive up the mountain to honor the appointment with the North Hawaiian Hospice Center in the small town of Waimea. I surmise that any chance I may have to get to Heaven will be aided by starting the ascent from the clouds of a mountain. Lord knows I need all the help I can get. The voice in my head is saying, "Better take a long ladder."

Rhett jumps onto the back seat. His tail wags and his large liquid brown eyes scan for something new. Wouldn't it be a wonderful world if we were all like dogs, waking up every morning positive, looking for something new, and wagging our tails anticipating the day?

Have I done the right thing coming to Hawaii? Consumed with the vision of what a peaceful death should be helps take my mind off the reality of my finality, also called premeditated avoidance.

I have burned the bridge back to my former life. Note to self: If you ever get the chance again to burn a bridge, try not to be standing on the damn thing.

Eckhart Tolle teaches us to be aware of our negative feelings. "Don't judge them, define them, or try to stop them. Just observe them and allow the feelings to dissipate." Or something like that.

The drive up the mountain to Waimea, a small town of 7,500, is pleasant. With little traffic on this two-lane road, we ride at a slow pace dictated by the numerous curves. My eyes traverse the ascending fields as they coalesce from golden brown to lush green. The car's front windows are hidden in their door frame, allowing nature's thermostat to lower the temperature as we go higher. Waimea has a dry side and a wet side. Don't we all?

This little town, crowned with low hanging cloud cover, has a McDonald's that serves a breakfast of spam and eggs. Bet you can't get that in Hoboken, New Jersey.

I tell Rhett, "Stay cool in the car when I go to the hospice office and there will be a treat of spam and eggs in your immediate future." He has no idea what I am offering other than he does know what "treat" brings, proven by perked ears and swishing tail.

Hawaiians consume more spam than any other populace in the world. They got hooked on it during the second world war as a meat substitute. The detox center in Hawaii can help you with your addictions to alcohol, heroin, and crack cocaine, but there is no recovery program for being hooked on spam.

A can of spam has more sodium than the Bonneville salt flats. Hawaiians are said to live longer than other Americans; some say it is the lifestyle. I say it's because they are pickled in sodium.

Right before Waimea, we pass a B&B on the left that is set on lavish grounds where it is said to have entertained famous people from around the world. Only a few houses reside on each side of the mountain road, but none close together. Up ahead is the sign "North Hawaii Hospice." There are two small olive-colored metal buildings surrounded by a garden of Eden flora with palm trees big and tall. The buildings are for the Hospice administration. There are no beds at the North Hawaii Hospice Center. This hospice functions as an at-home care service.

There is a calm vibe upon entering their driveway. This serene vibration must flow in part from the staff and their mission to lovingly assist in making the transition from life.

After parking, I leave Rhett in the Rogue SUV with instructions not to bark at anyone nearing the vehicle and repeat my bribe of spam and eggs. He looks at me like "What?" He is probably thinking, we gave up everything and traveled 4,000 miles for spam? I left out the word "treat" because, like Pavlov's dog, the word rings a bell in his head that causes him to jump around like a dancing chicken on a hot plate. That utterance equates in his world to instant gratification.

Sensing the energy of the hospice grounds or my tone of voice, Rhett settles quietly on the back seat, his head between his front paws. I hope he is not pouting.

The receptionist welcomes me warmly and guides me to a small conference room where I am to meet the hospice director, Ms. Mariah Dodd.

Ms. Dodd quietly walks in. She is tall with brown hair, brown compassionate eyes, and a comforting smile. She takes my hand in both of hers and says, "Please call me Mariah." I swear there are angels singing.

We get right down to how Max Largent will make the transfer from life to death as peacefully as possible.

"Dr. Grossman has submitted the required forms," she says. "You are approved to be under hospice care when it is time." Which is her delicate way to say, "It's life's last call; you don't have to go home, but you can't stay here." At least she didn't flicker the lights on and off as she said it.

Signing the forms giving the hospice the authority to care for and cremate me, means I just agreed to make an ash out of myself.

Mariah. I like her name. "One request, please. When I do flatline on the life support machine would you please pull the plug, wait ten seconds, and then plug me back in to see if I reboot?"

She laughs with a smile the Heavens ordained, mission accomplished.

She is beautiful, so I can blame life's circumstances for being exposed at this moment to the Largent curse of being much too glib in front of attractive women. My joy and burden in life is I have never met an unattractive woman. I also find this current impulse to attempt to be charming somewhat reassuring that I am not dead yet.

We then address two concerns. "I have no immediate family and I would like to die in peace and alone."

With a knowing smile she looks into my eyes and quietly says, "Your request is not that unusual. Some people desire to die alone to the point of hanging on until the family leaves the room."

"That's comforting, thank you. I did bring my best friend with me, and he will need a home after I am gone. Can your organization help with that?"

A little confused, she said, "We have never had that request before."

"Sorry, his name is Rhett, and he is an eight-year-old long-haired German Shepherd, but please don't tell him because he has never been told he is a dog, and it may be too much for his sensitive self."

"When your time is near, we will have someone from our staff come and spend time with Rhett so he will have some familiarity and hopefully make his adjustment a little easier." Then she adds, in a reassuring tone that seems to permeate in the death industry, "Max, if you don't find him a new home, we will."

"Thank you. If it is at all possible, I would like to meet whoever might take him."

"We will start putting out the word for candidates."

"I would like to add the name of Jane Gay, a lady at the Kona Veterinarian Service. They have a connection."

She writes that down. Then, with a smile that would make a dead man blush, she states, "Don't worry about Rhett. From our experience, dogs are much easier to place in a new home than pigs and parrots."

Hey, who is glib now?

I inform her that Rhett would not be a burden on anyone, not only is he sweet and loyal he has a trust fund to pay all the expenses for him to live out his days in the style he is accustomed to. His trust will be administered by a friend in Houston who will contact you.

With a laugh of, 'I can't wait to tell this at our next board meeting' she replies, "That's another first."

I want to say, "There are many firsts with Max Largent," but I remind myself I am not here to impress and to stay on point. The point being these fine folks are the last living beings I will gaze upon as I close these lifeless green eyes.

"Mr. Largent."

"Max, please, I don't want to die with strangers."

She smiles. "Don't be surprised if Rhett doesn't leave your bedside as animals sense their owner's release of life."

I laugh. "Rhett has never left my bedside."

She nods like she understands. I bet she has a dog.

She unfolds a brown leather portfolio and writes the names and phone numbers of two at-home nursing services on the Island.

My crazy mind wonders if it is possible to arrange for a 20-year-old French home care provider named Fifi.

Don't say it. DO NOT say it! Dammit! Don't be glib to the person who will decide when to pull the plug.

After handing me the name and numbers, Mariah says, "There are several folks who come to Hawaii to die. Some check into a hotel to await their end without telling anyone of their plan. That causes many problems for family, friends, funeral homes and, of course, the hotel."

I blurt out, "Maybe they croaked when presented with the mini-bar bill?"

Dadgum! I can't help myself even when trying to help myself. I am what I am. So, what if she doesn't like me? What's she going to do, not pull the plug? Hey, I can't let these golden glib opportunities slide by. That's like sending a fastball down the center of the plate and asking Mickey Mantle not to swing at the second one.

Praise the Lord she laughs and at my request then gives me the name of a crematorium.

Taking this info seriously, I say, "I would like to pay someone to spread my ashes on the waters of Hapuna Beach with Rhett there."

"That is a divine location to leave the world. Whatever you would like us to do, please put it in writing."

I follow up with, "Here is the contact information of Mr. Baker." Saying 'Mr. Baker' in my Southern accent brings another sweet smile to her lovely, sun-kissed face. "Billy Bob will make payment for your services and all expenses, plus arrange to collect any personal effects."

Miracle of miracles, I have finally discovered a beautiful woman who does not say, "Oh I know Billy Bob"—but she will.

Our business finished, she walks me to the front door and as we are about to shake hands, I ask, "Would you like to meet the infamous Rhett?"

With delight she says, "Absolutely."

Mariah and I walk across the gravel parking area to the car, hearing the rhythmic assurances of our feet crunching gravel. The sun is intermittently peeking through and around low-hanging drifting clouds of white and gray. The breeze is mellow and the lush green vegetation says, "You're in God's hands." Then it hits me. For the first time on my weird journey to find peace while crossing over to the other side of life, I realize that it's going to be okay. For me and for Rhett because we will be guided and supported by good caring people.

Before we reach the car, Chief Barks-A-Lot, who has moved to the front seat, surprisingly just sticks his head out of the window, wags his black and brown tail, and doesn't bark. Probably thinking he didn't want to ruin his chance at a spam sandwich.

"Oh what a beautiful, sweet dog." She pats his big head which he uses to follow her hand so as not to miss a single touch.

"Please," I plead, "I have to live with him the rest of the day." Turning my attention to Rhett, I add, "As for you my fine furry friend, don't let this go to your big head. She found out you have a trust fund."

Mariah laughs. "Don't worry about Rhett. He will have a loving home."

With tears of relief about to come over me, I quickly go to shake her hand.

Having none of that formality, Mariah gives me a hug. It's all I can do to hold it together in the parking lot of North Hawaii Hospice.

Slowly parting from her caring embrace and keeping my head down so she can't see tears welling up, I walk around to the driver's side of the car and slide in. Rhett knows something is different and he quietly lays down. Peeking out of the corner of a moist right eye, I have a glance of her walking back to her world of caring for strangers in need of comfort.

I didn't tell her, but I will have Billy Bob make a donation including my watch and other valuables to the North Hawaiian Hospice Center.

They are now my family.

40

NIGHT BRINGS THE LIGHT

It is dark and I like it. Night is when everything is possible.

The clear night sky feels like being covered by a soft, black sheet with pinholes that sparkle. Then there is the moon, God's lighthouse, a steady beacon that changes size every night but is always there to guide you home.

These Hawaiian night skies are aided by local laws requiring that streetlights be pointed downward so as not to dim God's canvas.

Lying in this lounge chair, I can touch Heaven.

Being one with my environment and thus able to be alone with thoughts, which can be soothing or scary. Tonight, let's choose soothing. This is the tricky part—controlling my thoughts. Do I create conflict within myself about why I moved 4,000 miles away with weeks to live? Why do I have to die so soon? What could I have done better with my life? Why didn't I find true love? Why didn't Kim Basinger fall in love with me even though we never met? Why didn't I win the damn lottery? If you're going to ask negatively charged questions, be a bear about it. Heck, be a grizzly and inquire about all the obtuse remembrances that live in a cluttered unsettled mind.

Not tonight, Max. No mental gymnastics on this heavenly Hawaiian night. No questions, no answers. Just be. Let's save the mundane and the whimsical for the daylight. Nighttime is the right time for repose, where everything is new again.

I am the judge and jury of my life. Nobody else gets a vote or has a say. Maybe a quote or an opinion, but they and their judgments don't count. As I lie covered in a wreath of peace on this tropical night, I enjoy the warm breeze across my arms and face. Knowing my last breath might be taken while lying on this lanai gives me solace. As does gazing up at the night sky with a hand resting on Rhett's soft back and feeling like Kim Basinger loves me and I just won the lottery.

Fatigue sneaks in. Tumultuous dreams from today's nap drain me. I dreamed I had three cars and could not find one. When I did find a car, it wouldn't start, and I didn't have the money to get it fixed.

Why can't I dream about wild passion with the purpose to please instead of lost or broken automobiles? Is it about not being in control? I'm always looking for a way out, even in my dreams. I'm going to make a deal with my guides and angels tonight to allow me to dream about being in a car—that starts.

With my luck I'll dream about the night in my senior year of high school, petting with my girlfriend Janie in a blue Chevy with fogged windows, parked on a dark, dead-end street with teenage hormones raging.

I whispered, "Would you like to get in the back seat?"

She replied, "No, I'd rather stay up here with you."

One of the nicest and wisest rejections I ever experienced.

4 1

SHOCK AND AWE

It's been eight days since the meeting at North Hawaii Hospice and yesterday I finally got around to calling the nursing service for an at-home care interview. I have been resting, taking barefoot walks around the manicured lawn, and enjoying the peace. When the energy is cooperating, telling my life story in a recorder in hopes someone would want to hear it. If not, then at least it provides a conduit for good memories.

The afternoon siesta reminds me how as a rambunctious boy I dreaded those summertime forced naps. Now, they are as welcome as a long-lost playmate.

The doorbell rings. So much for naps in paradise.

I have forgotten, the at-home nursing service is coming today. Oh well. I put on a tee-shirt and shorts, shuffling in bare feet to the door. There is a shock as I open the door and behold a beautiful ghost from the past. The Hawaiian sun accents a face with young unblemished skin, eyes hidden by black sunglasses with a gold Chanel logo. She is also sporting a silver and gold Rolex watch.

What nurse can afford such accessories?

She removes the expensive sunglasses, exhibiting her emerald, green eyes. She is around five foot seven and has full lips protected by clear lip balm and perfectly white teeth all accented by a slightly sunburned face. I am envious of the sun.

Have I seen her before? It can't be possible, but she looks so familiar.

Hanging from her brown shoulders is a yellow sundress imprinted with white flowers. Light brown leather sandals accentuate slim sun-enhanced ankles and calves. Wearing no make-up, she personifies youth, beauty, and innocence.

If this is going to be my nurse, I want to hang on longer than the heavy hand of cancer allows.

She is holding neither a purse nor notebook. And it's not just me smitten with this mystery lady; Rhett immediately moves past me and nuzzles her right leg. She instinctively pats his head. So much for having a ferocious guard dog.

"Hi, are you from the Big Island Nursing Service?" I ask.

"No," she says with a focused stare.

I must look like I'm trying to figure out Chinese arithmetic. I ask, "Okay. Do I know you?"

"No, you don't know me. I am your daughter."

I am usually a glib kind of guy, quick on the trigger with a comeback, but at this moment John Maxwell Largent, wide-eyed with shallow breath, is at a loss for words.

Not caring about my being confused, she continues in a tone someone might use when delivering a cold pizza to your door, knowing there is no tip at this address on this day.

My heart races like a scared small animal. My mind is numb as this beautiful young woman stares through me, but then it hits me: She looks exactly like a woman I knew 22 years ago. Maybe this is her ghost. Please let it be a ghost or too much pain medication.

At that moment Rhett wags his tail and moves even closer to her, which Chief-Barks-A-Lot has never done with a stranger before. I stand there, my eyes blinking like a hostage trying to send a distress message by Morse code. Shock is when you are suddenly told you have a daughter you never knew of and your only thought is, "Is there an angry mother far behind?"

She gives me a temporary emotional shock absorber by asking, "May I come in?"

"Of course, of course. Please do," I stammer. "I am sorry my manners are being weighed down by surprise. Please excuse me and the four-legged greeter rubbing up against your leg."

Finally, she smiles, but not at me, and pats Rhett. She reaches out to shake my hand. "I am Michelle."

Trying not to stutter, I say, "His name is Rhett, and I am Max." I catch myself. "You obviously know that."

She ignores my nervous stare and with a smile looks at Rhett. "Yes, I know your name—and Rhett's." She touches his appreciative head.

With a determined walk, she enters the living room where I am about to hear what I have been living without for 20-some odd years. There is no mistake who her mother is, but there is something about that look she is giving me that makes me think deep in there somewhere I see a part of me. Poor child.

She gazes out the full-length windows. "You have an amazing view."

"Thank you." Not being able to take my eyes away from her, I am acting like a freshman at fraternity rush week afraid I am going to say the wrong thing.

We sit across from each other on the two identical brown leather sofas. Rhett lies on the floor by my couch. I ask, "What's your last name?" I wonder if it is Largent.

"Miller," she replies. "My father died two years ago in a car accident."

"I'm very sorry."

"You haven't asked who my mother is."

"One doesn't have to be Inspector Clouseau to know that."

With a puzzled look, she says, "Who is Inspector Clouseau?"

"He's the main character in the movie series, *The Pink Panther*."

"Oh, yeah. When I was little Mom would make me watch those. She found them so funny, and I found them silly, but I would laugh, especially at the pratfalls."

With a far-off gaze like she is searching for a fond lost memory, she says, "I loved the scene when Clouseau spun this huge world globe, put his hand on it, and fell spinning to the floor."

"Me too. I watched every one of those silly movies just to hear her laugh. And what a wonderful infectious laugh it is. I would hear it and feel her joy. Does she still have that full laugh?"

"Yes, but she is not laughing much these days."

That's one minefield I will tiptoe around. "So, Diane Boyd is your mother?"

"Yes, that is her maiden name."

Her demeanor and direct answers make me feel like we are in a deposition where one wrong answer will doom me.

"And what a fair maiden she was." I'm trying to bring in a little levity. It doesn't work. This stranger, who just happens to be my biological daughter, doesn't laugh at my attempt at humor.

I try another tactic to elicit a friendly response. "Is her malady you being here?"

"You could say that" she dryly responds.

"How long have you known?" I start to say, 'that I am your biological father' but I cautiously ask, "Of our connection?"

"Right after my father's death. My grandmother told me. I guess she thought it would ease my sorrow."

Quick. An opening to change the subject to collect my

equilibrium. Speaking at too fast a clip I say, "How is your grandmother? She was always kind to me even when your mother was angry with my behavior, which I might add was always justified."

Good one, Max. Speak well of grandma and take up for mother.

With a look that says 'Is he working me?' she replies, "Grandmother is well and still as feisty as ever."

She has her guard so high I am surprised she could get through the front door.

Thinking out loud, which is not thinking but instead nerves, I say, "I guess your grandmother was doing what she thought was best to make you feel better. Which I am sure it didn't."

"How would you know?"

Dammit to hell. Just what I need, some angry kid complicating my dying in peace mission. I have uprooted my life, spent all this money to pass in peace only to be tracked down by an angry 20-something whose mother didn't want me in her life before she was born. Here it is again, the "all about me" mentality, but if you can't be self-centered about your last days on earth when can you? Stop. Calm the you know what down. Let go of the "it's all about me BS."

"Well, I know because at 12 years of age I was informed by a well-meaning inebriated aunt that the man I called father was in fact not, and that my last name wasn't Jameson but Largent. I was angry, hurt, and confused."

She doesn't say anything, so I change the subject. "How did you find me?"

"Uncle Billy Bob told me you were here and had a terminal illness."

First shock, now awe—as in awe s**t. Reeling on my figurative emotional heels.

"You're speaking of Billy Bob Baker of Houston?"

Another seismic disturbance because he is the singular Billy Bob I know, which makes him the only Billy Bob Baker I told I was headed to Hawaii. This brilliant piece of deduction makes me the Pink Red-faced Panther.

Then it hits me like a world record on an emotional Richter scale of life: this is the reason he came to my house to tell me he was burdened by a secret but had promised someone he wouldn't tell. When I told him to honor his commitment there was no inkling it was to Diane or about my only child. No wonder he left town so quickly.

"Uncle Billy Bob?" He kept this beautiful being from me all these years. She notices my change in mood—and crimson face.

"Please," she says. "Don't get upset with Uncle Billy Bob."

"Billy Bob Baker is not your uncle."

"He is like an uncle. I call him that because he has always been in my life and he's one of my mother's dearest friends."

I want to shout, "He is every woman's dearest friend" but refrain.

Leaning back on the couch, my eyes look to the wooden ceiling for an answer to these shocking revelations. I take two deep breaths then lower this aching head to see her staring with concern.

"Are you okay?"

Quietly I say, "Not to worry; I have cancer, not a heart condition."

Swaying slightly from side to side she twirls a strand of blond hair with her right index finger, an obvious nervous tick. Which she inherited from her mom, causing photo flashes in my head of an amazing lovely young woman that meant the world to me.

"Mother made Billy Bob promise never to tell you about me, so give him some credit for keeping his word."

"To your mother," I say, with blood not boiling but simmering. I debate whether to tell her about Billy Bob's last visit but decide what is shared between friends is sacrosanct even if that friend's action—or in this case non-action—really pisses me off.

Trying to appear calm, I say, "I wouldn't say Billy Bob is an original, but there was only one of him on the Ark."

She smiles at that.

Thank goodness, a smile. Billy Bob was always good for bringing a grin to a pretty woman's face.

"After my grandmother told me about you, she said, 'If you want to know anything more, go ask Billy Bob.'"

"Your grandmother was always kind to me, but leave it to her to bring the storm and then take away the umbrella."

She smiles and nods. The first thing we've agreed upon.

"I waited until last year and when I approached him all he would say was, 'Ask your mother.' I am sure he didn't want to cross her. Mom wouldn't talk about your relationship. All she said was, 'We were both young and in love and while I can never say anything untoward about Max, I did what I thought was best for me and you.'"

Must still be in shock because all I can say is, "She said 'untoward'?"

With a sheepish grin, she nods her youthful head. "I didn't want to deal with finding out more, thinking there was plenty of time—until ten days ago when Uncle Billy Bob called and told me of your health issues."

That is the last thing asked of him. "Please don't tell anyone I am dying." As sure as there are steers in Texas, when confronted with his—in my opinion—duplicity, he is going to invoke the "Billy Bob Baker mitigating circumstances" excuse of, "Max, you know I can't say 'no' to a beautiful woman." or some such BS.

"Are you mad I came here?"

"No, being mad is a luxury I can't afford." I search for stable ground in our shaky introduction. "When I met my biological father he was cold and indifferent. You won't get that from me, but may I ask, what do you want from me?" As soon as those words fell out, I sensed it was a bad move. If I had to write down all my dumb choices of words in the wrong moments, it would make Tolstoy's *War and Peace* look like an essay.

She flares up. "I don't want anything from you. I have a trust fund that more than takes care of my needs."

I shift on the couch from being uncomfortable, and I don't mean my bottom.

Feeling sheepish after being sheared by her temper, I backpedal. "That's not what I meant. I am unhinged by Diane and Billy Bob keeping something so important from me." I feel like a steel ball in a pinball machine that is bumping up against all sorts of flashing obstacles.

"I know this can't be easy for you. Allow me to rephrase the question. Is there anything I can do to assist in this situation?" Now I sound like an undertaker.

"I just want to get to know you a little," she says. "Who are you? And why did my mother leave you? She said she didn't tell you she was pregnant or that she was leaving." With green eyes glaring and lips pursed she continues. "And she is upset with Grandmother, and now me, for coming here."

"Sounds like the Miller women and Grandma have a lot to work on."

She shakes her head in an 'if you only knew' response.

"Would you like some water or juice?"

"If it isn't any trouble."

I know she is being polite but if she thinks getting water

from the kitchen is trouble, there is a whole new world about to open to her innocent eyes.

"Excuse me and I'll do the honors. Please feel free to look around." I head toward the kitchen. "I am sure Rhett would love to escort you."

He wags his tail at hearing his name.

I don't want water, only a reason at this moment to move and try to think. She has her mother's beauty, but she may have my temper and thousand-yard stare. Lord help us all.

Through the open doors, I watch her walk out to the lanai and onto the grass with Rhett at her side. She moves with the grace of a ballerina and self-awareness that defies her youth. Even in my confusion, I can still dig down and be in awe, the good kind of awe. She takes her shoes off and wiggles her toes. To feel grounded? What do I know about why she is barefoot on the grass? Then she does a slight twirl that causes Rhett to circle around her in delight. Is she shaking off the tension of this moment or announcing to herself, "I *can* handle this."

It's all I can do to keep any semblance of equilibrium while these ghosts of my past are competing with the present. Score: Past one, present zero.

"Not now." I sense the presence of my nemesis, the Devil. I say, "Don't you dare come around when she is here, or you can forget your book. I will not care what you do to me." He must have heard, for the chill is gone.

Calming down, I pour the water into two glasses, make a decision, and pray it won't be the mistake of my life. But it must be done.

42

GOD'S INFINITY POOL

I join Michelle outside. Holding our tumblers of water, we stand with Rhett between us. We are enthralled by the view of the ocean's vast horizon that offers us a reprieve from this awkward first meeting. Though nervous of misspeaking and upsetting her, I put fear aside; she has come a long way for answers to troubling questions.

To break the silence I ask, "How do you like God's infinity pool?"

"Makes one feel small."

In a soft voice to honor the moment I say, "In this massive universe everyone's world is small; it just doesn't feel that way."

"Like now?"

Smart kid. "Can't get more immediate than now."

The proverbial first meeting's ice is melting as we both recognize each other's discomfort, and that we may have more in common than DNA.

Feeling her beginning to relax and praying not to come across as insensitive I say, "As mentioned earlier, I know you are going through a lot. Your father dies, and then you discover your biological father is someone else. Now you find this stranger has the unmitigated gall to be dying thousands of miles away. The only good in that is an uptick in your air miles."

She smiles, which makes me want to. If she did inherit my defensive, quick-to-anger temperament, hopefully it came with a little sense of humor.

Continuing to speak in a soft tone. "Not having much time left means I can't afford the luxury of being vague and putting important things off, which I have been excellent at in the past, so please allow me this moment of clarity. I am glad you are here and do admire your courage."

She turns and stares right at me with those penetrating eyes, sending the clear signal of 'Be careful what you say, Max Largent.'

"What I hope you understand is that I don't have the strength or ability to deal with anger. Mine or anyone else's."

Still making eye contact—my God this girl is tough—she looks as if she is thinking, 'I came all the way for this?'

I gesture to the lounge chair. "May we sit for a little while?" I don't give a reason, but I am sure it is easy to see I am fading. The past few minutes have taken an energetic toll on both of us. I would verbalize that, but based on her youth, she will say, "Duh, you think so?"

With her bare feet and slender legs, Michelle moves with finesse to the cushioned lounge chair and I, like a cow getting into a canoe, fall into mine.

Rhett follows her. The faithful dog has become smitten by a beautiful stranger.

Changing the subject I ask, "How long have you been on the Big Island?"

"This is my third day."

Wondering why it took her three days to see me, I ask, "Do you like it here?"

Somewhat guarded, she says, "Haven't seen much of the Island; I've been hanging out at the hotel beach."

"What hotel?" I look at this beautiful young lady that I pray is blessed with few scars and fresh eyes.

"I am staying at the Hapuna Beach Prince Hotel."

"Very nice. One of the Island's best," I say. Michelle has her mother's sense of style and a budget to match. Diane is proof a woman doesn't have to be born into wealth to enjoy and appreciate nice things. Not being born into wealth and privilege can be a distinct advantage because it prevents the affliction of living a life burdened with a false sense of entitlement.

"That would be my choice, beautiful beach and breathtaking open-air lobby." Small talk aside, I continue. "I need you to please think about something important."

"Important to you or me?"

"For both of us. Just trying to say, it's meaningful to me to depart this world in peace. So, please take your time and think about how we can interact within the calm spirit of this island. If for any reason you don't think that is possible—and I will understand—I'll give you my email address where you can send any questions. I do feel fortunate we have met."

Stumbled through that the best I could.

She looks away. "Let me get back to you."

The girl has more maturity than her mother and I at her age. Part of that must be in today's world of social media and politics which is every day and all day in their faces. Young adults today are forced to mature in a hurry or get lost in the spin cycle of instant, insane negativity.

Not wanting her to leave on such a serious note, I say, "I hope you take the time to explore the island. This slice of Heaven is a spiritual place and encourages deep reflection. Plus, even the ugly guys here are healthy-looking."

She laughs. "I had a sense of that the first day."

"Excellent." I smile. "There is a ritual you may want to try. As you watch the setting sun, request that it take your cares of the day over the horizon. That is something we can share even if we are not together."

She puts her shoes on and the three of us walk to the living room where I give her my card with my mobile number and email address. We take a slow walk out the front door and down the flat stone path to her rental car, a blue Honda.

Standing by the car she scans me, Rhett, the house, and the view of the ocean, seeming to take one last picture for her memory bank or trying to decide if she wants to come back. She reaches down and pets Rhett and he moves closer.

I'm confused, I don't know whether to shake her hand or give her a hug. A handshake might say, *Let's keep our distance*, whereas a hug may say, *I hope you come back*. I remember the promise just made that I would not treat her as my father had treated me, and so with her permission I give a gentle hug.

"Michelle please remember, your mother did the best she could with the information she had at the time."

With wide eyes, she replies, "That sounds like something Mom would say."

"Yes, but it doesn't mean it's not true."

Her smile is like her mother's when she was happy or when she discovered something new. On a spur-of-the-moment long weekend trip to Naples, Florida, we made a point to be on the beach every evening at sunset. The only thing more beautiful than God's curtain going down on the day was the look on Diane's face as she stood in wonder. Spontaneity being my ruling compass, we took an unplanned driving trip from Naples to Key West. My selling point to Diane was, "You think the sunset on the ocean is great then wait 'till you see the sunrise ease little by little up from the edge of the ocean's vast horizon. It's like you are witnessing the earth's creation. Bring you closer to the Creator."

The journey added five hours of driving time to the 13 hours back to Nashville from Naples. I would have driven farther than the southernmost tip of the United States to gaze upon Diane's look of wonder during sunrise on the ocean. There are no pictures of that trip except for the ones tattooed on my soul.

Once in Key West, after we toured Duval Street and Hemingway's House, Tennessee Williams' small home, and walked past the too many tee-shirt shops and bars, we retired early to our motel on the edge of town since we had to be up before O-God-hundred. In the early morning dark, we stopped by a Cuban coffee stand that was doing a brisk business to early risers headed to their work in kitchens and fishing boats. With espresso in hand, we sat on the cool white sand and watched the greatest show on earth. I love my quick memories of special times in my life. After I got back from Santa Fe, New Mexico I took a trip with the sole purpose of trying to forget Diane leaving me. I drove back to Key West with the idea to spend a couple of months being Ernest Hemingway. I got the drinking and fishing part down but not the writing. When the drinking didn't stand in the way of functioning like trying to put on my pants, I would sit on the same beach with an espresso from the same Cuban coffee stand watching the same magnificent sun taking its time to peek up from earth's edge and pretend she was still beside me and try not to cry. If anyone ever threatened to torture me, they would hear, "You are wasting your time; I do better a job than anyone ever could, every bloody day and night. I am classified under 'if they ever go to brainwash him it would be a light rinse.'

I am rambling but have to stop because Michelle is looking at me like, "Are you going to say anything?"

I pay her a compliment. "As we say in the south, 'Your mama and daddy did really good.'"

She laughs.

With that, she pets an approving Rhett one last time and gets into the car. She circles the drive past three palm trees, the two-car garage, and lava rock border wall. I see a slender tanned hand slide out of the window waving. I pray it is saying, "So long, for now."

43

IT'S NOT YOU, BUCKAROO

I didn't cry when Crazy Mama died. She made it easy; she instructed, "You are not to cry when I am gone." She demanded no funeral, no memorial service, and no mention in the obituary section of the newspaper. Her exact instructions were followed. It's called still controlling from the grave.

I justified the lack of tears for Mother's demise with a Southern cliché: "She is in a better place." In her case, that could have been Walmart since Walmart always made her feel superior, especially on Halloween.

I fall on the couch. Rhett lays at my feet. I feel like the eighth caller in a seven-caller contest; my call was answered with, "We have a winner, and it is not you, buckaroo."

Looking out the window, I follow the sunlight to the horizon while fighting a losing battle against tears. But why tears? Is it because I never knew I was a father? Never knowing the life-confirming thrill of holding my own child? Or that Diane didn't trust me to be a husband much less a father? That I never had the opportunity to know someone who would love me for me? Screw it. "I'll take Double Jeopardy, Alex, for Life's Lost Opportunities." I am so tired.

The tears are here, it's an involuntary release. Like most men, I hate crying. You have a scrunched-up prune for a face, make sobbing noises that would scare a bear, and the salty tears take the starch out of being. There is no resistance to these feelings of loss. I can only observe these uninvited visitors, just get out of the way as they follow their own sad course.

I have to acknowledge the courage it took Diane to have a baby without a father, start her life over in a strange city, and raise what appears to be a wonderful young woman.

With my self-centered insistence for no drama, it may have driven Michelle away never to return. This attitude is rationalized by thinking it can be made up to her by answering any questions *via* email, the modern-day Cowardly Lion.

"Hey Max, sounds like you're having a pity party. I love those. Let's invite all your friends. O that's right; you don't have any friends. What a pity." Then the diabolical laugh.

Shaking off this intrusion, I head outside to see if the ocean breeze can clear a muddled head.

In Hawaii, it's the custom not to wear shoes in the house. A sanitary practice brought by the Japanese from their homeland. I walk out through the lanai and onto the grass. There is wind on receptive skin, sun lighting the way, pliable turf under clinging toes, and dried tears on a tired face. Just keep pushing those thoughts and people away, Max, like you have everyone. You don't have the strength to contemplate what could have been 22 years ago or even 22 minutes ago. I sound like the Devil.

I deprogram these unwanted thoughts by focusing on the view.

The line of sight is altered by rooftops and palm trees in the distance. After that, it's all the way to the limitless Pacific

Ocean. Out in the distance, there are white caps on the water which could mean a storm is brewing. I sincerely hope so since there are few things better in life than an easy downpour on a warm tropical day. Nothing is better to clear the mind than sitting on a lanai, hearing raindrops on a tile roof, watching them cascade down wooden columns, and hearing the rain's rhythmic landing on self-created puddles announced to one and all, everything is clean.

Standing here longing and looking for answers that may never come. Swaying back and forth, eyes closed, hugging this battered body because you do whatever it takes to feel good about yourself, even if it's going to Walmart on Halloween.

THIS EVENING'S FARE was a modest meal of prosciutto and melon on toast. It's a cloudy night with no artificial light to blind me to the darkness.

Lying on the lounge chair, feet extended, I watch Rhett's contented eyes illuminate the dark and recall Diane and the sweet memories, occasionally interrupted by the unanswerable "why?" We were both always circling each other, trying to guess what the other was thinking, but we were too scared to find out—also called a "push/pull relationship." One gets close, the other pulls away, and vice versa. A do-si-do dance where everyone ends up 'changing partners.'

Not being able to communicate and trust has ended more relationships than booze, infidelity and leaving the toilet seat up. I know.

While wondering if Michelle will call tomorrow I head for bed, followed by my second shadow and memories.

4 4

YOU AGAIN

The rains came after dark and gently rock me to sleep.

"Max, Oh Max!"

That son-of-a- . . .! At 2:00 AM, it's the Devil.

I bolt upright in bed; it would do no good to bolt out the door. He is everywhere.

Turning on the light next to the bed causes Rhett to look at me, and my loyal dog must be thinking, "Here we go again, talking to himself."

"What? What now man?" I demand. "Don't you know what time it is?"

"No," he says. "I don't have a watch. Maybe I'll get one of those Apple watches. One of those with a black face and black band that goes with my black Armani suit. I, the Devil, don't need a watch. It's my time all the time. Don't you just love it?"

"No! I do not love it! What do you want now? If it's about the book it's finished. I have left instructions for it to be edited and published if I don't make it in time."

"Good job, Max. I am concerned that you don't have much time."

"Are you concerned for me or for your book?"

"Max. Max, Max, after all our stimulating time together and you have to ask that question? Of course, it's about the book.

"Be sure to leave instructions that there is only one editor, for every editor, there are different opinions. Five editors equal five opinions. If the Bible had two editors for every chapter we would still be waiting on the New Testament.

"If what you have written is everything we talked about then I will like it, especially how we used your life as an example of what not to do."

"I am so glad that I have led a life the Devil can use on what not to do."

"Get over that self-pity; it's not becoming. There isn't a life lived that I can't at some point say, 'Just like I would have done.'

"Again, why did you wake me?"

"To brag, didn't I say, 'You have one more shock coming before you die?'"

"Yes, you did, but I was hoping it was a cure for this brain tumor."

"Sorry, Max. Miracles are in God's hands, and She has decided your time is up."

"Okay, you made your point. I don't have the will or strength to deal with you."

With anger in his already dark voice, he says, "Deal with me? You humans *deal* with me every day and when you don't have the courage to find the grace of God, I win. So don't think for one moment that just because you have written a book you are unique in dealing with the Devil."

"Please, please leave me alone so I can die in peace."

"Largent, I am out of here, the book is finished and so are we. Why spend any more time with a soul so self-obsessed, they are blind to the fact that pointing out the obstacles in their life were guide-posts to discover a new ending of life on earth.

"Your desire to die in peace now has more to do with how

you handle the situation with your daughter than me or my book. It will be fun to watch how you screw that up.

"Goodbye Max. Can't say 'it hasn't been real' Here is a parting gift. Remember what I said about having the courage to find God?"

"Of course. You just said it."

"Don't tell anyone or put it in the book, but if you have the will and grace to find God, you don't need courage."

"Wait, wait!"

"I thought you wanted me to go?"

"I do, but you owe me."

"Owe you what?" He asks incredulously.

"I finished the book. At least tell me if my soul is going to spend eternity in Hell."

"That's not *the* question you should ask."

"Then what, in the name of all that is holy *is* the question I should ask?"

"Is there a Devil?"

45

THE NEXT DAY

Every night the doors in the bedroom are open. The full-length glass frames open the threshold to a blissful night air that is so soft you can wrap presents with it. The salty current of air flows over me and says, 'sleep easy'.

Rhett enjoys his all-access pass to nature, allowing for a potty break anytime he feels the urge. All I do upon waking is locate his act of nature and pick up the evidence with a plastic bag. When in the world did we start picking up dog poop? Sidewalks and public spaces sure, but in our own yards? I should be giddy he is not a pony.

I prepare his food bowl, pour fresh water, and we take a short stroll around the yard. He likes our confined outings on the grass as it is just us and no leash. Too soon someone else is going to have to perform these missions of love. Lord, I pray they are a gentle soul. Instead of complaining or worrying, I stay in the moment by being grateful I can still bend over. Whoa, time out. This being in the moment and gratitude for picking up dog droppings is a little much, even for a dying man.

Rhett knows our time together is limited. I catch him gazing at me longer than normal like he is trying to figure out what strange event has taken over our once comfortable routine of a life and am I okay. He is always by my side. In the past, if he saw me head to the bath or another room he would raise his head, make sure that's where I was headed, then lay back down and close his eyes. Unless my destination was the kitchen, then he would have walked through fire to where his treats are kept. His hyper-vigilance started when my symptoms first started.

The best I can do is love him and make sure he has a loving home. I hope his new home has another sweet dog, so he'll never be alone. The stories he could tell his new friend. Wagging his tail in greeting when his new friend will ask "Rhett where you from?"

"Nashville, Tennessee."

"How in the world did you get all the way to Hawaii?"

"I had this owner I loved very much but he was one crazy dude."

Since we have been in Hawaii, Rhett has deviated from sleeping by the bedroom door to lying next to me in bed all night.

I turn on the computer and delete emails that should have been unsubscribed. Thank goodness there are no messages from folks I didn't tell I was leaving or of my condition. It is nice to know you don't have to start the day lying or ignoring. Just an email from Billy Bob wanting to know "If my trip was uneventful," which is a cowardly way to ask, "Have you met the daughter you never knew you had that has slipped my mind to tell you for only 22 years of friendship?" Not wanting to give him the relief of knowing, I did what comes second nature: I play dumb. "Thanks for asking, all uneventful, will be in touch."

Should I call Billy Bob to inform him, "I am pissed off at you" or "Thank you."? I do neither. He was squirming the last time I saw him on his surprise visit to share his quandary of needing to tell me something he promised not to tell me. Then benevolent

Max let the big guppy off the hook. Now his super-secret is known; let him wiggle a little bit, but not long.

That afternoon there is a phone call from area code 713 but it's not Billy Bob's number. I answer, expecting to hear airport background noise and Michelle saying, "*Sayonara.*"

"Max?"

"Hi, Michelle."

"I have been thinking," she says in a voice that is balanced, neither high nor low nor fast, like she had been practicing what she is about to say.

Amazing how long a dying man can hold his breath.

"You are correct. I don't have the right to vent my anger on you."

"Michelle, I should have been more understanding of you. I am sorry."

"Please let me finish."

"Okay, sorry." I keep saying that.

"I have given a lot of thought to what you said about coming all this way to be at peace, and I called Mom."

I want to ask how that went but think better of it. She is not the only smart one.

"If it is not going to disturb what time you have left," she pauses too long on that word. "I would like to visit again to get to know you. Besides, I think Rhett and I have got a thing going."

Deflect with humor. Wonder where she got that?

"Michelle, I would like that. I hope you will allow me to get to know you a little too."

"Deal," she says.

"Tomorrow morning there is a Farmers Market in Waimea. If you'd like to go, please be here around 9:00 AM and we will drive up. It's a great drive-up, but the drive-down is even better. Do you have a light jacket?"

"Yes, a windbreaker."

"Perfect. It could be damp and cool that time of day."

"See you then."

"And Michelle."

"Yes?"

"Thank you."

"Thank you, Max." I can hear her smile.

4 6

THE FARMERS MARKET

Michelle arrives at 9:15 AM. I am excited and apprehensive about being with her while Rhett is excited about riding in the car. Rhett loves riding if it's not to the vet's office.

I perform a personal miracle—staying quiet while Michelle takes in the view of the mountain, cattle, trees, tall grass, and low-hanging clouds. Rhett hangs his head out the window for that windblown look he loves so much.

We pass the North Hawaiian Hospice offices. I notice Michelle looking at their sign but neither of us speaks of it. This is a new day and a new beginning of a hopeful connection, at least on my part.

Just past the Parker Ranch School on the left I pull into the Cowboy Restaurant parking lot. The Parker Ranch School is a private school where kids from around the world come to be educated far from home. The Farmers Market uses an adjoining field with picturesque views of the cloud-capped mountains, providing a cool foggy morning. You feel you are on top of the world. And you are.

We walk into the Cowboy Restaurant and order coffee to go and to ask permission to park there while we go to the market.

Not out of fear of being towed, but that instant karma thing is always on a short timers' mind.

"Can you get me an Americano coffee?" she asks.

I grin. "This is not a coffee shop in some mall, so how about a Hawaiian coffee?"

"What's that?"

"Coffee made with 100 percent Kona beans grown about 30 miles from here."

"Whatever," she says, sounding like a young woman who is used to getting what she asks for and is disappointed when she doesn't. Ah, the burdens of being an only child from a well-to-do family.

With Rhett on a leash held by Michelle and Kona coffee in our hands, we walk across the gravel lot to the Waimea Farmers Market.

I take a moment to be in the moment: A cup of hot coffee in my less than warm hands on a brisk morning, children running around excited and laughing about being outside with their friends, having a big-time sugar rush from fresh pastries. We move among a rainbow of colors from the tents giving shelter to the merchants of creativity offering pottery, knives, paintings, colorful flowers, fruits and vegetables, honey, and jams. The scent of fresh bread and sweet sticky buns lingers in the air. The grass that provides the carpet for this weekly event smells freshly cut.

The first tent we enter is occupied by Barbara, a shining white-haired, green-eyed lady with generous lips, a perfect smile and soulful energy that says, "All is right in her world." If we are lucky, today she might share a little of that world.

Every Saturday morning from the town of Hilo, Barbara drives her blue Chrysler van filled with creations of color—handmade bowls, plates, pitchers, and mugs. Barbara has the long delicate slender fingers of an Artist. How do I know all this? Last Saturday Barbara sold me a sunburst red and midnight blue coffee mug. To buy anything new shows how much my subconscious was seeking an energy like hers.

Every morning when I hold her artistry with both hands, I am comforted. Okay, I know, you're thinking, "Come on Max, it's just a coffee mug." True. But in times like these, it is a solace to simplify.

I introduce Barbara to Michelle, but without mentioning our relationship because I didn't know how Michelle wanted to be addressed by me to others.

Michelle takes her time perusing Barbara's wares, looking at them with an artist's gaze. She refrains from making a purchase but says, "I'll be back next week." Barbara appears to believe her, that knowing thing where two women can communicate with just a look.

We continue our slow stroll, allowing our senses to guide us among the tents. On the right, we pass a knife maker and a women's clothing tent with handmade blouses and skirts swaying on hangers reminding one of International Flag Day. There is an Island jam and honey company, a fresh local vegetable vendor, a juice booth, a tent of sweets, and of course a local coffee company all with signs that proclaim, "We ship." At the center of the market is a bakery truck with a long line. We are stimulated by a cornucopia of exhilarating sights, smells, and sounds.

Not for the first time I notice a few young men about Michelle's age looking her way. I didn't see her looking back but it did stir a protective emotion. Good thing for her I was not there when she had her first date. I would not have said a word, just sat quietly in the back seat of his car cleaning my gun.

Pointing to the bakery truck I proclaim, "Love their olive

bread." We find an unoccupied picnic table and sit. "Let's enjoy our coffee and wait for the line to go down and talk about whatever you'd like."

We sit facing each other and Rhett settles under the table beside Michelle.

I ask, "May we take a moment to just feel and see where we are? I take as many of these timeouts as I can, they are comforting."

"Of course," she says.

I gaze up at the lush mountain, feel the slight mist on my face, and notice the smiling families. Every child is laughing, except for the little guy who dropped his chocolate ice cream cone and is crying because a dog is eating his treat. His mother assures him, "They make more."

I look at Michelle and take in her long blonde hair barely moving with the breeze. Those green eyes must make the Hawaiian hills jealous. Her beautiful smile fills my heart with joy— and sadness. The joy of seeing something I had a part in bringing into this world but the sadness of never being part of that world. I think of something I read: "She is every tick of every clock." Time is standing still.

I am thankful for this moment.

Smiling at her I say, "Thanks for that."

I know she is thinking I said thank you for the quiet moment but that thank you was for far more than she realizes.

"Whatever questions you have," I say, "just shoot. Come to think of it, you are the first woman I ever said 'Just shoot' to, because some would gladly have taken me up on it."

I want to begin her question session by getting her to grin. It doesn't work.

She asks, "You said, 'every time you come here'. Have you been to this island before?"

"Yes, this is my fifth time."

"So, you didn't just throw a dart at a map and say, 'This is it'?"

"Nah, and be glad I didn't, or we might be sitting in Kathmandu." She still wears that poker face, so I am more direct. "I consider this island my spiritual home."

Looking as if she's trying to figure out what I mean she changes the subject. "What about that silver bracelet you are always wearing?"

Oh good, a question I can answer without all my internal organs slamming shut.

"After your mom left Nashville for Houston, I decided to go to Santa Fe, New Mexico to clear my head and mend my heart. It was there I came to understand my problems were emotional boomerangs that keep coming back to hit me no matter how far I threw the darn things away. I came to realize it is not where you're at, it is where your head is.

"When you don't have the courage or wisdom to look within yourself for the answers to your pain, you keep looking outside yourself, be it geographical, a liquor bottle or pills, or in another person. I am a loner and the pull of the New Mexico desert and isolation felt appealing at the time."

"Did you drink much in Santa Fe?"

"Why would you ask that?"

"Mom said you had a tendency to drink, especially on weekends, and that sometimes you were fun and funny, and sometimes you would go into a dark place no one could enter."

"I didn't have a drinking problem. I had a thinking problem. In those days, I thought I had to be bad to have a good time. Some people drink to feel, and others drink to bury feelings. I subscribed to both, but when the pain was intense I refrained from drinking because it highlighted and empowered the pain

"That sounds smart," she replies.

I shift on the steady wooden bench, even the soulful cloudy view, the laughing children, the smell of fresh soaps and warm bread can't keep me from being uncomfortable. Attempting to reveal hidden emotions I have kept in . . . my subconscious, I wonder: Would I be this open if I weren't dying?

"Smart had nothing to do with it," I reply. "In those days, I drank to push my feelings deeper rather than face them."

"That must have been deep."

"Cold, too. Drinking made dark places darker. So, to survive, I stayed away from drink until I could make it on my own."

"Were you mean when you drank too much?"

"Not unless you were a male who crossed me. Then you paid for my father's indifference. When I had one Tequila, I had a good time; two Tequilas, everybody had a good time; three Tequilas, nobody had a good time."

"Is that how you got that scar on your chin?"

"Yes."

"You must have been a good fighter," she says.

"The guy with the scars is not the good fighter, it's the other guy." My philosophy of scars and fighters brings a smile to her beautiful face, which now makes those long-ago battles born of ignorance worth it

Continuing to answer her question about the bracelet, I say, "I was in the Santa Fe town square where the natives—and I mean the real natives, not the rich, jewelry store owners or would-be Georgia O'Keeffe artists, but the New Mexico native jewelry artists who sat on their colorful blankets, spread on the sidewalk under a wooden overhang across from the historic downtown park—sell their crafts. I was looking for a ring with a bear emblem because I have an affinity for big ol' grizzly bears being that they are one of the loners of the animal kingdom. Later I read that on a subconscious level bears represent a longing for a father's energy."

She asks, "Being a father or having one?"

That rocked me on my heels —and I am sitting down. Looking across the grounds, past the schoolyard up the hillside, past the homes sparsely situated on high, all the way up to at the smoky mountainside and frantically seeing no way out I reply, "Good question but my self-awareness didn't go deep enough then to fathom that I didn't love myself."

No response other than staring into my eyes.

Letting this intense moment hang in the cool air I say, "Back to the bracelet. After asking several artists if they had a ring with a bear symbol I was directed to a Hispanic silversmith's stand across the street in the park. He sold me this solid silver bracelet with 13 thirteen bear paws that he had created. I have worn it every day since. This bracelet and Rhett are the two things I would never sell or give away."

"From what little I know from grandmother, Uncle Billy Bob, and even Mom, your animal symbol should have been a turtle," she says.

That puzzles me. "Why is that?"

"Mom says you built a hard shell around yourself, and while that is a safe place to hide from the world, there has never been room for anyone else."

Just what I need, a 22-year-old stranger psychoanalyzing me with 22-year-old information. Stay calm. No need to be defensive or upset; she is just looking for answers.

"Your mom may be on to something, but I still prefer to be thought of as a bear. Some days I am a teddy and some days I am a grizzly."

"Well Two-Bears-Largent, I don't think I want to be around the grizzly side."

"Smart," I say, which is a veiled signal to move on.

She looks at the bracelet. "Do the 13 bear paws have a meaning?"

"Yes. That's all the silversmith had room for."

I get a look that says, "Smartass."

I slide the bracelet off and pass it to her. She balances it in her palm and says, "It's heavy."

"Yes, due to the price of silver these days; jewelry is not made that heavy anymore."

"You have had this as long as I have been alive?"

"Every day."

She avoids my gaze and hands back the bracelet then changes the subject. "There seems to be a lot of happy people here."

"Yes, most Hawaiians are laid back, but some young ones have a problem with drugs. I like to believe it is no worse than anywhere else."

People stroll around us, smiling and greeting friends, children doing what they do best, running and laughing, and dogs checking out other dogs. It looks like one big happy Hawaiian family reunion without the roasted pig. Rhett lies under the table by Michelle's feet acting like he's on vacation and has met a new friend.

"How did you meet my mom?"

I immediately look to see if the bakery line has gone down, no such rescue. Obviously, her mother didn't tell her. "I was working as a foreman's assistant for an earth-moving company and your mom was the secretary for the developer of the project. Each afternoon I would take the equipment timesheets into her office, which was the highlight of my day. She was beautiful and nice, plus her smile was the highlight of my day."

"How did you get her to go out with you? I can't see Mom ever dating a construction worker."

"She was transfixed with my looks, charm, intelligence, humor, and hard hat—but most of all, my humility."

She smiles.

"I told her I was from royalty and was working construction in Nashville for my gap year."

We both laugh.

"I really don't know why your mom let me into her world, which was so foreign to me. She came from a good, loving family, and she went to private school. I went to a high school where when you raised your hand in class, the teacher didn't know if you knew the answer or had a knife at your back.

"I think your mom was attracted to me because I was different, you might say a free spirit, which in those days usually meant one didn't have a job. But be it ever-so-humble, I did. At the time Diane saw more potential in me than I did.

"I owe her more than I could ever repay. She not only made me want to be a better man, but she also allowed me to believe I could." I bow my head feeling a warm sensation of a forgotten memory.

She asks, "How is that?"

"When I met your mom, all I wanted to be was a bulldozer operator, which, don't get me wrong, is an honorable profession and you don't have to work when it rains. But Diane knew it was not my passion. With her encouragement, I went to a University of Tennessee adult education center at night and took real estate courses. From there I got a job as a property manager for an office building developer. Then a year later I started my own company. Two years after that Diane moved to Houston."

"Let me ask you, Max, when you look at me do you see me or see my mother?"

"Michelle, I really want to give you the right answer here, so why don't you help me out?"

"I am serious."

"I know you are, just buying a little time so I can give you the proper answer. You obviously look just like her and for that, we both should be grateful. When I see you smile it stirs some warm ghost of my past and for a moment I get to visit the beauty and bliss of the first-time love that came into my adult life. I believe the only thing we can control in life is our attitude, and when it comes to Diane and others I choose to recall the good. When I look at you and hear you, I see and hear only you. You are unique and beautiful in your own way, and I want to learn more about the real you. Does that answer your question?"

"It's a start."

Lord help me!

FIND SOMEONE WHO WILL LOVE YOU FOREVER

Standing in line at the bakery truck we are blessed with the olfactory perception of home, gifted by freshly baked bread. I order olive loaf for me and raisin bread for Michelle.

Tempted by the apple turnovers I get two. When your days are numbered there's no need to count calories.

The drive down the mountain from Waimea is as I had hoped. We glide the curved road with the ocean in the distance. Michelle remarks, "Coming out of the clouds into the sun is beautiful."

"If you like this, I will take on a ride you will love."

Halfway down I turn right onto Highway 250 heading to the little town of Hawi which is basically the long way back to the house. The locals call Highway 250 the upper road, but since there is more than one upper road I use the tourist designation.

At 3,000 feet, I pull left onto a graveled lookout which allows a full view of the coastline past the Hapuna Prince Hotel to where you can almost see the airport. The town of Hilo on the other side of the Island is the most populous, but Kona is considered by many as the capital of the Big Island, not for legislative reasons but because it has the only Costco.

After a quiet moment of absorbing the view—or does it absorb us?—we proceed to Hawi. As with any idyllic virgin road traveled you gladly surrender your focus, we remain quiet. I sense Michelle taking in the green landscape on both sides of the tree-lined road. There are cattle farms, riding stables, open fields with hovering clouds that remind you of picture postcards of Ireland. She is taking all this in with an artist's creative eyes.

Green landscapes give permission to one's brain waves to cycle in the relaxing state of theta where artists dwell to create. To honor her commune with nature at thirty miles an hour, I engage my most difficult challenge, other than listening to rap music; staying quiet bestowing the gift of not by being His Royal Glibness.

The distant views, and amazing landscapes proclaim, "God really loves these Hawaiian people for they live in Heaven now." With no time frame to get to where we are going, this is the ultimate road trip—which I get to share with my biological daughter.

Biological father. Biological daughter. Sounds like a disease where we both have to wear a hazmat suit. Until we feel totally safe with each other that may not be a bad idea.

We slowly cruise into the town of Hawi, pronounced HA-Vee.

Hawi is a town of about 1,000 folks that was a commercial center for a now-closed sugar plantation. Closed plantation is Hawaiian for 'we can't get folks to do backbreaking labor for slave wages anymore.'

There are churches, a school, two grocery stores, a real estate office, and the ubiquitous souvenir shops. Souvenir shops in Hawaii are where the Chinese and Japanese tourists come to buy stuff that is made in China and Japan.

We find a parking space a block away from our destination, the Bamboo Restaurant; it is a busy lunch hour. We leave Rhett in the car with the windows down. He sulks in the back seat.

"He seems very quiet back there," Michelle says.

"The last time I was here I told him he should stay in the car because the Bamboo was a Vietnamese restaurant and they served dog."

"That is not true!" she says.

"Of course not; they serve cat."

"I don't believe you."

"Proves you are smarter than Rhett." I look back at Rhett. "It's not Vietnamese and they do make a great hamburger." Into the infamous Bamboo Restaurant and Bar we venture.

If you want the feel of Hawaii in the 1950s or '60s, go to the Bamboo Restaurant. It's a wooden building built between 1911 and 1915 as a hotel, later to become a dry goods store, and now a restaurant, art gallery and, surprise-surprise, a souvenir shop with all things Hawaiian. There is a wooden sidewalk that leads to wooden screen doors. High ceiling lights covered in shades with frills hanging that you know your great-grandmother had. Most everything is wood—tables, chairs, floor, and large windows—taking you so far back that you think you are in an old John Wayne movie about Hawaii. Not likely to see a fight in this bar unless you count the very large hula dancers struggling to move their ample backsides to the rhythm of the ukulele.

This true Hawaiian establishment has good food, drinks served in replicas of coconut shells and the *Aloha* Spirit.

We're met by a friendly waitress, which is common in Hawaii but a minor miracle because just about everyone here must work two or three jobs just to stay afloat. They deal with tourists all day and night, and we know how unpleasant and demanding some false sense of entitlement jerks can be. Like leaving your hometown and a ten percent tip gives you permission to be rude and demanding. That's usually the ones that just arrived. You find after a few days most tourists mellow out and as the surfers say, "Hang loose."

When the kings ruled there was only one penalty, if you broke the law then you died. Now they can't kill you for being rude, but they can and will give you the "stinky eye" and, like every restaurant in the world, do things back in the kitchen to your food you don't even want to think about. With that, I smile and ask the waitress her name. She reciprocates with a bright as a summer day grin. "I'm Lisa." I introduce her to Michelle and give her my name all out of common courtesy—and fear of what she can do back in the kitchen.

"Why did you introduce us to the waitress?" Michelle asks once she takes our order.

"Out of respect. You can tell a lot about a person's character by the way he or she treats wait staff. I never understood the logic of offending someone who handles your food."

We settle in while we wait for our hamburgers and her fries. I tell her, "Fried food is harder for me to digest these days but, like a former lover, I do fondly recall our time together."

Speaking of past loves, she asks, "You were only married that one time to a country music singer?"

I nod.

"Didn't last long, did it?"

"Nope. I kind of suspected it wouldn't because when we said our wedding vows she promised to love and cherish me for the gestation period of a gerbil."

I think that went over her head. Or she wants to ignore it because she replies, "Sure, but why did you marry her?"

"We had only been dating for three months when Miss Mona Lou called and woke me at 1:00 AM while she was on the road and told me that it was going to be in the paper that morning, we were getting married in four weeks."

"Hard to back out of that, I would think."

"Yep. Especially at that hour." Hope the food comes quickly to fill up my mouth with something besides indigestible words. "I could have and should have found a way not to go through with the wedding. It would have been embarrassing but not as much as it turned out to be."

"Was it because she was famous and beautiful and the excitement of being married to someone like that?"

"Very astute but the real reason is something I have never told anyone." That gets her attention. "Mona was the first person to ever make me feel nurtured."

"Not even your own mother?"

"Least of all her. Mona was older and she was very attuned to other people's needs and she picked up on mine quicker than a hiccup. Bottom line is, I have to take responsibility for my part because I was immature and definitely not self-aware."

"How did it end?"

"Not well. I was due to pick her up at the airport but sent her assistant since I was in a meeting. Because I wasn't there, she got on another flight. Her assistant handed me a note at 2:00 PM that it was over. Then it was on the local 5:00 PM news that we were getting a divorce. I didn't see her for seven years and only then in passing at a restaurant."

"Not even in divorce court?"

"Nope. She had a fan in a local judge, and it was over."

"That must have hurt?" Looking a little sheepish, she realizes that sounded obvious.

"I was hurt and embarrassed for a long time, and I should have been."

"So. what do you recommend?"

"Don't do what I did?"

"Not to worry."

"Good."

"Good that you won't worry?"

"No. Good, our food is here."

I get to pause. This doesn't help my appetite but if I don't eat, she might feel bad about bringing up something I don't like to dwell on.

"The abandonment was the hard part. I was nurtured and then abandoned again in my life, so it just reinforced my lack of trust issues with love. I take responsibility for my part."

"Turn the page?" she asks.

"Turn the page."

"Any other regrets?"

"I never got to see the baby gerbil."

"Max," she says sarcastically.

"It could be worse; I could be sarcastic."

"Funny, not!"

"But true. Yes?"

"Uncle Billy Bob says you have known a lot of women."

Why does that uncle thing make me want to cringe? "As in the biblical, 'He knew her well'?"

"I guess," she says with an expression like, that was too much information.

"More than most. Not as much as many."

Lisa came by with more tea. I make sure to smile even though my food is safely in front of me. Hey, even the paranoid have enemies.

"So, what have you learned about love?"

"When you walk into a room and you see that guy and all the bells and whistles come banging so loud your head spins and you think, *this is the one, he is it,* run."

"Why?"

"Because that is your subconscious picking up on his subconscious that this guy has all the issues I have with my father, my last boyfriend, or myself, and here is my chance to heal them."

"Is that why my girlfriends keep picking the same type of assholes with the same results?"

"You kiss your mother with that mouth?"

She slings it right back at me. "Yes."

"Sounds like your girlfriends are trying to heal themselves thinking they can heal someone else. Point being, we can't heal anyone else. How can we know the answer to someone else's problem if we can't pass our own emotional quiz? As a qualifier, if that same dude is willing to work on his issues and you are willing to work on yours and the urge to merge is still strong, give it a go."

"The urge to merge?" Even when she cringes, she is beautiful.

"Sorry, dating myself here." I take a sip of tea. "Another important thing about healing is that children can't redeem their parents. Try as we might there is nothing you can do to fix your parents and make whatever issues they had in negative parenting right. Again, heal yourself and don't pass it on."

"Grandmother said you never had a father."

"True. I now realize that was an emotional crutch I used for so long, it made me a cripple in trusting people."

Looking like that is as far as she wants to take this, she asks, "What else in the matters of the heart, O' wise one?"

"You want your money back for this sage advice?"

She laughs. "No, but I am buying lunch."

"Okay." I am too tired to argue with such an independent soul. "The second and most important advice is, now listen up—"

"You want a drum roll, Max?"

"Just listen because it is important. Find someone who will love you forever and when forever is over will be kind."

"That sounds cynical."

"Maybe to you." She doesn't like that. "We all are looking for a soft place to fall."

Her eyes open wide, and she looks like she just discovered a secret. "Is that why you are in Hawaii?"

Finally, somebody understands.

"Back to 'sounds cynical.' There is nothing better than the first six weeks of a romance, but the passion will wane. The excitement hopefully will slide into comfort. Find someone with a good heart who will be kind even in bad times. As Joseph Campbell said, 'Love is perfect kindness.'"

"Who is Joseph Campbell?"

"He taught comparative religion and mythology at Sarah Lawrence College. His writings were the inspiration for *Star Wars*."

"Okay."

I pause and savor a sip of tea. "Also make sure you have a good heart; it takes two."

"I have a good heart."

"I believe that." I smile proudly as if I had something to do with it. "Oh yeah, also make sure before you marry that he is a good roommate."

"A good roommate?"

"Do you want to be picking up after him all the time? Does he leave the toilet seat down? And don't fall into the trap a lot of women do and think you can train him. The only misconception greater than 'the groom will change' is that the bride won't."

"Did you make a good roommate?"

"Of course not. It was all an unconscious and often selfish effort to stay single, or as your Uncle Billy Bob would say, 'I don't want to be number one to one; I want to be number two to ten.'

"Did you have anyone you really loved?"

That causes a pause, aided by the sunburned faces and legs of a family of four—leaving the adjoining table with the racket of a jailbreak, obviously tourists. With their plastic bags of souvenirs, colorful tee-shirts and tank tops, wrinkled shorts, flip flops attacking the wooden floor, chairs shuffling and reeking of suntan location. They loudly debate whether to go swimming or shopping. From the weary weathered look on the parents' faces it appears the swimmers won.

"Besides your mother?"

"Yes." Her eyes desert mine as she shifts down to her food.

She doesn't want to hear that, but it is true. I hope she is not holding 'what if' thoughts in her young head. A little bit of that is natural but too much of that can ruin your days and nights. Says he who is the master of the 'if only.'

"There were two others."

"Care to talk about them?"

"Nope."

"Why?"

"It makes me sad."

"That's honest."

"Thank you."

"May I at least ask why none of those relationships lasted?"

"I didn't love myself. I was very lucky three times in my life because I have known three women who had the wings to fly over the wall I built around my heart. Those are the loves that light my life."

"Even if you couldn't love yourself."

"I said I was lucky in those days. I didn't say aware."

"All men are lucky. Take the most miserable bastard in the world and there will be some woman somewhere that will love him."

"You sure you kiss your mother with that mouth?"

"Not in an exceedingly long time."

Note to self: The girl is tough, competitive, and doesn't forget.

I am compelled to leave her guideposts so she can find her path in life an easier journey.

It is a desire to leave a part of myself that is good and provide some reason for my time on earth.

"Michelle, sometimes the worst vice is advice but please find a man who loves himself or wants to. By no stretch of the imagination am I smarter than you, but I have been on an interesting journey so allow me to share with you a few of the things I have learned. If they don't resonate at this time they will later." I smile. "Or they won't."

"I am listening and, believe it or not, interested."

I shift my weight and try to remember what I was about to say. "Good, a very important skill in a relationship is to learn how to fight intelligently. Falling in love comes naturally to most. Must be, since a whole lot of folks seem to keep jumping into it. Knowing how to disagree without being disagreeable means at least one of you must be an adult. A little thing like when you are really mad and need to go cool off, tell your partner, 'I am really upset right now and I need time to settle down, but I will be back.'"

"What good is that?" She looks at me like I am a man from Mars.

"Saying, 'I will be back' will avoid abandonment issues for the other person. Plus, it will give you time to go into your quiet place to find the right words to annihilate him to his core."

"Really?"

"Only if you want the relationship over."

"Did you know how to fight intelligently?"

"Of course not. None of what I share with you is a 'should.' I dislike those, and the people who are a firehouse of unsolicited advice. They are usually insecure know-it-alls who don't practice what they preach."

"Wow, easy Max. I now know what pushes your buttons."

"Sorry. Got carried away. I have so many buttons I could start a shirt factory." I laugh. "Just want you to have an easier experience in life."

She replies, "Isn't experience supposed to be a dear teacher?"

"Yes, and it is mostly a fool's school."

"Where did you learn all this?" she asks.

"I didn't learn it. I lived it." I notice the volume of chatter rising with the tide of tourists, locals, and hustling staff. We are seated by a large window facing the front porch and the two-lane street.

Michelle puts down her burger. "Look!" Lo and behold, a Hawaiian cowboy with a worn ball cap, faded jeans, and aged cowboy boots is seated on an old western saddle atop a tired brown horse ambling down the middle of the street in Hawaiian time. Michelle finds this scene amusing since she is from Texas.

I volunteer, "Like I told you. A one-horse town."

Watching her laugh is a joy. It is not as full-throated as mine and is slightly more demure as I remember her mom's. Sometimes the ghosts that stir in your mind can be friendly and welcome.

I cough and cough again, a nagging noise which is disconcerting. Too bad I am not going to make it into old age and end up in a home for the extremely elderly and nearly dead. I will be their most entertaining codger. "Just sit Mr. Largent in a corner by himself with his bib and Depends. He still remembers his old dumb jokes and will sit there, laughing, chuckling, and grinning and have such a jolly time."

Instead, I say, "I will close this session on love with, 'Don't love a man just for what he is, but love him for what he wants to be.'"

Looking more puzzled than when she saw the cowboy and horse parading in the middle of the street, she says, "Why is that?"

"It means he is aware."

48

REVENGE IS OVERRATED

As we finished our meal and our new friend Lisa cleared the table, I felt compelled to ask Michelle, "Ever been hurt by someone you trusted?"

Looking puzzled she replies, "Why do you ask?"

"I don't know, just came up in my head,"

"Not really. Sure, I had high school and college heartache, girlfriends hurting my sensitive feelings, silly stuff like that."

"Don't worry about your sensitive feelings. Between me and your mother, it is your birthright." I raise my eyebrows and get a small smile from her. "Anyone can hurt you, but it is up to you if they harm you. With words or deeds anyone can cause you pain and our first inclinations are to hurt them back so they will never do that again. It's as if the first time they hurt me it is their fault; the second time it is mine. That knowledge is more painful than the first hurt because you have no one else to blame. Everybody is going to hurt somebody sometime, unintentionally or intentionally. I have learned the hard way that I do more harm by holding onto my pain than the harm done by the original sin or sinner. It's like holding burning coal in your hand and thinking it is hurting someone else. Albert Einstein, whom I have heard was a fairly smart person, said, 'Weak people revenge, Strong people forgive, Intelligent people ignore.' Let it go."

"How do you let it go?" she asks.

"Awareness. In that moment of hurt and anger you don't have to be on the same lower level as the sorry you know what. Sometimes a sense of self-importance can be invigorating."

"Isn't that being judgmental?"

"I prefer to think of it as observation. As in, 'That fellow is a world-class jerk. Not judging, just making an observation.'"

"But revenge can sometimes feel so good," she says.

"True, if you know no other way to relieve your pain. But it is playing a game that has no winner. That, my dear, is a circle that will not be unbroken. If you really want revenge and nothing else will satisfy you, do the cruelest thing you can do to someone like that."

"What is that?" she asks enthusiastically.

"Be happy. It drives them crazy. Nothing drives a mean or heedless person crazier than to know their actions have no consequence on your state of mind."

"Can you do that?" she asks.

"I can now, but I wasted years doing it the hard way. Now you don't have to. I have had family abandon me in times of need, friends cheat me and throw away long friendships for a few thousand dollars, and I have been cheated on."

"You?"

"Yes, and everybody else out there has had it happen in one way or another. Life is an elevator that does not always go up and when those down buttons of yours are pushed by someone else, remember only you can control how far that is. Do you hit the pause button or continue to let your emotional elevator drop? The good news is you can be in control of your feelings about what happens in life by being aware of them and knowing negativity is like the weather. In comes a dark cloud. Think okay, cloudy today but sunny tomorrow."

She says, "Are you saying that tomorrow is another day, Scarlett?"

"Hey, don't let Rhett hear you make fun of Miss Scarlett." I smile and continue. "Don't waste time avoiding your feelings, just accept them. As Eckhart Tolle says, and I'm paraphrasing here, 'Deep acceptance relieves pain because you have nothing to fight against, nothing to resist.'"

She widens her eyes and says, "Max, I don't know if I can do that."

"Not to worry. You will know when it feels natural."

"What if it never does?"

"That will be okay."

"Cute."

"No, seriously, Michelle. Whatever happens, you will always be safe."

"I have to think about that," she says, looking like she doesn't exactly believe it, get it, or relate.

That's alright, hopefully, she will be able to store these nuggets of my late-in-life so-called wisdom in a quickly accessible corner of her mind that will help her when needed.

"Max, I don't know about all this, especially the forgiveness or no revenge thing."

"I understand. You will be fine even if you don't use it. Besides, that revenge philosophy was not to protect you, it's for the poor soul that ever crosses you."

She laughs. "Now that is the best thing you have said. Have you always been so philosophical?"

"You mean boring?" I laugh. "I have always been interested in learning the whys of life and gathered bits of information along the way, but I didn't start cramming until I realized my final exam was near."

Looking down I continue. "But speaking of boring, it is said, 'There is nothing more boring than a born-again sinner.' I am not born again in the modern religious parlance, but I have been a sinner, some of which I enjoyed. Hey, if you can't enjoy a few of your sins, why do them?"

"I don't think you could ever be boring." With that, she asked for the check, which she picked up.

I really need to lighten up, but I feel rushed to help her even if it's from some of the eye-opening conversations with the Devil. I need to share what I have come to learn so I can help her know the Max Largent of now and not the lost soul of the past? Maybe all this is to help me justify my negative experiences in life? This 'needing to feel significant' thing keeps popping up.

Am I still looking for ways to find significance in this life? It's like always looking for the sign 'this way home' while standing in your house. How's that for, *whatever happens is okay*?

After Michelle pays the check, which I thank her for, we take a slight detour and meander through the art gallery and gift shop sections of the restaurant. I notice she focuses on the local artist rather than the gifts.

I ask, "What do you think of the artists?"

"Love the settings of the ones on the water. A couple of these local arts are quite good."

"I am having a watercolor teacher come by the house for another private lesson in two days.

Looking surprised, she says, "You are taking water-color lessons? Why?"

"The marble won't get here from Italy in time to do my masterpiece sculpture." I smile but she looks stunned. "It is beautiful and peaceful here, but I need to focus my mind while I can on something creative, probably not going to be able to finish it but I believe you are never too ill or crazy to try something new, other than maybe skydiving."

She smiles at that. Which is all the reward I need at this moment in my life.

I have spent the best part of my life trying to get women to like me or to laugh. Now I get to try and make a pretty woman, one that I have been part of giving birth to, laugh. I feel as if I have been sitting on the bench of life and in the last few minutes of the game and the coach is finally putting me in to score the winning touchdown.

We walk slowly back to the car as my breathing is getting difficult and fatigue is setting in, but I try not to show it by stopping to gaze into the windows of shops along the way. At a small jewelry store, our reflection in the window has the faded image of two ghosts side by side, one tall looking like he is close to the end of his life's journey, the other young and vibrant just beginning hers. It's the only photo I have of us.

These two blocks feel like two miles on a bumpy road. At the car, Rhett is happy to see Michelle and maybe me. Starting to get jealous.

I am tired and should ask her to drive the 25 minutes to the house on Highway 270, the Akoni Pule Highway. But this is her first trip down the mountain from Hawi and the coastal view is so memorable, I want to bask in her wonder.

The coastline is on the right, the passenger's side. We pass farms, isolated homes, wind turbines. Farther south we are close to the entrance of State Park Puukohola Heiau. These sacred grounds are situated back from the cliff's edge with views of the Pacific Ocean. A stone structure built by King Kamehameha is said to have taken thousands of men passing large stones hand over hand. I am not physically able to take her but I do hope that soon she will visit this sacred place. There is a plaque that quotes King Kamehameha when he dedicated this holy site to his people, "Endless is the good I have given you to enjoy."

    I have made this majestic drive many times and each time experience serenity. Today above all others. My tired, achy body predicts this will be the only opportunity to partake of this view with Michelle. I am floating home as time stands at attention and salutes our passing, for 'Endless is the good she has given me to enjoy.'

49

RIGHTEOUS

We arrive at the rental house around 2:00 PM. It has been a wonderful day of sharing and getting to know each other but my stamina is waning.

"Michelle, I am sorry, but I have to take a nap. You are welcome to stay while I do so."

"I would like to go to the beach for a while. May I come back this evening?"

"That would be great. I'll go down the hill and get the best fish tacos that a girl from Texas ever had."

"Sounds good. Say around six tonight?"

"Perfect."

"Max, would you like for me to take Rhett for a walk before I go?"

"Yes, that is kind. While you are at the beach I would like for you to please consider something." Hope that didn't sound pleading.

"Sure." She smiles while petting Rhett.

"I have three bedrooms and it will give us more quality time if you stay here. It just makes no sense to pay for a hotel room and drive back and forth. Please understand I don't expect you to help out or take care of me in any way—I have housekeeping and soon will have home nursing care."

"Do I get to walk Rhett?"

"That's taking care of him." I smile.

"That's not hard to think about. Sounds good to me."

"Please understand, I don't want you here at the end, that will be too hard on both of us."

There's that Largent DNA defensiveness on her pretty face. I have known that stare all my life.

"Don't you think that I should decide what is too hard on me?"

Oh boy, here we go. "Please just think about it. I am so tired you are dueling with an unarmed man."

"We'll talk tonight."

"Thanks," I say. "And by the way, I loved today."

She smiles. "Me too."

Rhett is doing his happy dance as Michelle picks up his leash. He is so damn easy. Men run from leashes; dogs run to them. Difference between feeling constrained and feeling let out.

I barely make it to the bedroom but find the energy to take my clothes off, get under one sheet, and let a healing breeze wash over my body. I am one large sail on this boat of a bed, and I have nothing to do but just be, sleep, and dream.

I sleep so hard I didn't hear Michelle bring Rhett in or sense him lying beside me.

After two hours I am surprised to wake up hungry so I make toast of olive bread along with caffeine-free tea.

I lazily stroll from the kitchen to the lanai, with the required Hawaiian uniform of the day—tee-shirt, cotton shorts, and bare feet. Under the shade of the lanai sunglasses are not needed. Besides, who would want to shade this view?

If I had lived here all my life, I would have been one brown laid back dude whose only ambition would be to have no ambition. Most likely would have only been stoned once, from September

1999 until today. Then when asked whether I have had a good life? I could honestly say, "I don't know. I got stoned and missed it."

Maybe it was best I visited paradise, not lived in it.

Here is a potential self-help book—*Being Productive in Paradise*. It would be a short one. The author would have an understandable excuse: "Sorry, too laid back today to write."

This mental wandering leads me to these surfer dudes in Santa Barbara California who had a house remodeling business called When the Surf's Not Up Construction Company. To know when they would knock off each day all their clients had to do was check for when "surf's up".

On the Big Island, I could have opened When the Sun's Not Out Real Estate Company. Would have made a lot of money on the rainy side in Hilo. Would have been broke and homeless in sunny North Kohala, but man, what a tan!

Gathering these scattered thoughts is like herding cats, I go back inside to shower then put on a fresh daily uniform. Being no slave to fashion these days leaves more time to hunt for my cleanest dirty shirt.

Rhett and I head downhill to the Kohala Burger and Taco Stand. Stand being the operative word because if you don't get one of the four small tables you are regulated to standing. The line is usually long but worth it. Reminds me of the Yogi Berra quote, "Nobody goes there, it's too crowded." I place the order and get the obligatory, "No problem, Bro." There is never a problem in Island living and everybody—male, female, or animal—are "Bro."

Most situations here are addressed as "No problem, Bro." You can be lying in a ditch on the side of the road with three gunshot wounds in your chest and the paramedics would ask, "Dude, you, okay?" only to barely hear "No problem, Bro."

The Hawaiian State slogan is *Ua Mau ke Ea o ka 'Aina i ka Pono*. Try saying that with a mouth full of poi. It means, "The life of the land is perpetual righteous" or "No Problem, Bro."

Pono means righteous. I have known this for years and now with Michelle here I feel it.

At the Kohala Burger and Taco Stand, the kitchen is hot and crowded and the tables too close for comfort, but everybody smiles—especially the dudes in the kitchen and the waitresses. This is living and dining island style.

I ordered and over-tip the friendly server because I was indoctrinated many years ago by an older wise waitress, "If you over-tip, you will go to Heaven." Not that I really believe that, but in my present situation I shall leave no stone of generosity unturned. Besides, the beautiful sincere smile of appreciation I receive is more than worth it. After the 10-minute drive back to the house, I watch the horizon with a calmness that whispers, "*Pono*".

50

BACK AT THE RANCH

Michelle should be here by now. I put on a collared shirt because of childhood discipline in "No eating at the table without a shirt young man." It's easier to put on a shirt than wonder why that clapper keeps ringing in this hollow head. Speaking of ringing, there is the bell and Rhett's wagging tail.

Opening the door, a vision awaits. Michelle wears a sky-blue sundress with small yellow flowers that highlight her blonde hair, white sandals that show the beginning of tan lines around her feet, and a scent of fresh soap and jasmine—all of which make my heart leap. No luggage. Maybe she just needs more time to think about my offer to stay—or not.

Rhett couldn't be happier if I had tied a pork chop to her leg.

"Come on in." I smile. "Red or white wine?"

"White please," she says while bending down to pet the lucky boy.

Late afternoon. Young beautiful girl in a sundress in Hawaii. What else is she going to drink? I open the wine that the real estate company left as a greeting. While Michelle and Rhett are on the lanai, I preheat the oven to warm the fish tacos.

I hand Michelle a glass of Chablis. "Glad you got here before sunset. It is the best show in town. And, you don't have to sit through one of the hotels' staged Luaus of poi, pig, poke, and other local foods that are way overpriced."

"I have never had poi," she says.

"Fresh poi is made from the tori root and can be tasty, but as it ages it tastes like that white paste you used in kindergarten."

"You ate paste in kindergarten?"

"Not on purpose or will I poi."

Sounding like she is looking forward to our meal, she asks, "Are we still having fish tacos?"

"Yes, and fresh guacamole and chips. There are so many avocado trees around here I think it is a codes violation not to have one or more in your yard."

The VOG is up tonight, not so much to affect one's breathing, thank God, but emitting enough gases to make for a spectacular sunset.

We sit, leaning back in our lounge chairs with ankles crossed on our blue-padded cushions. There is a small wooden table between us holding our beverages. Sprawled out in front of our chairs is Rhett as happy as a bird with two beaks.

On cue, the sun is starting its descent. As promised, the gases of the VOG have gifted us an awe-inspiring scene of vibrant colors, different shades of slate, purple, orange, and red that accent that big round white ball of a sun. It's a wonder we are not hit with a cover charge. At the end I wouldn't be surprised to hear a big booming voice say, "You have been a wonderful audience. Don't forget to tip your waiters and waitresses. Do drive safely. Goodnight!"

Not wanting to break the mood I don't ask whether she wants to move in. So, naturally, she brings it up. Amazing how easy it is to talk when you both have something else to focus on besides each other.

"Max."

Is that my name or the sound of the other shoe dropping?

"I have thought about your offer for me to stay here. I just don't know if I will be able to leave when you want me to."

"Why is that?"

"I lost my dad in a car accident, and I wasn't able to say goodbye. I don't know if I can do that twice."

"The doctors said it's possible that in the final stages of brain cancer the patient could be difficult and angry. But the good news is, then it won't be so hard to say goodbye."

"I am being serious here."

"I'm sorry, Michelle. When I don't know what to say. What I am deflecting is, I worry the last days for someone in my condition will not be a pretty sight. I have read that it may get to the point that someone will have to turn my head just to look at you. That is not the way I want to be remembered."

"Don't you think that should be my decision?"

I pause. Where are your jokes now, laughing boy? After a moment I say, "You are right. It's your call, but I do not want you taking care of me. There will be a nurse for that. Just promise me that you will stay only as long as you are glad you came."

"You mean leave now?"

"Now look at who is deflecting."

"May I ask one question, then I won't bring it up again."

"Sure," I say with the enthusiasm of a guy about to get a root canal. Nothing puts more fear in a man than a woman saying, "We need to talk."

"Why haven't you fought this?"

"I was too far gone when the diagnosis came in and no doctor could assure me survival was possible."

It's not totally true, but I am not about to tell this sensitive soul that I had no one at that time to suffer for. Some things in life are best untold.

"Sun is setting." I point to the horizon.

With that Michelle reaches across the small table and lays her hand on mine. This causes my eyes to blink, this is the most beautiful sunset in my life.

As the sun melts into the horizon, I say a prayer asking the sun to take away my cares of the day, and for the life of me at this moment I can't think of one.

We spend the evening eating fish tacos and talking about her school years and the Island and the easy energy.

"I would like to give staying here with Rhett and you a try."

Thank you, God.

I suggest she check out the Akamai Art Supply in Kona and stock up on what she needs to paint. A way for her to be entertained when I rest.

She looks at me with eyes filled with suspicion. "So, you checked out the art store assuming I would be staying?"

"Young lady, I learned a long time ago to never ever assume what a woman is thinking or going to do. Makes life a lot less complicated." Then with genuine gratitude, I add, "Thank you for giving us more time together."

With that, I give her a key to the front door. Yes, I leave the bedroom and living room doors open all night for the breeze but lock the front door. My theory is, if someone breaks in while I am here, I will give them all my money. If that is not enough, I will tell them, "I can write you a check."

We'll have to rethink open doors with Michelle here, but we will talk about that.

I start to ask what her mom said about her staying here, but don't.

"I will check out of the Hapuna Prince at 11:00 AM tomorrow and come on up."

Maybe it was wishful thinking on my part, but she seems pleased. Try not to muck this up, Max.

"Get room service in the morning," I say.

"Why?"

"Because the service here sucks."

She laughs. "That sounds like a princess problem."

Cool kid.

Rhett and I walk her to the car and watch her drive off into the night.

Lord, keep her safe. She is the best thing I've got going, except for this hairy, big-headed, tail-wagging, eating machine at my side.

I WAKE AT 10:00 AM after having slept well except for my usual medication-induced 2:00 AM feeding, *aka* peeing in Morse Code—dot, dash, dot, dash, dot, dot.

Michelle arrives around noon this Sunday with two suitcases and has her choice of the two guest rooms. She chooses the one in the front as it has its own door out to the yard and overlooks the ocean.

She will have to share a bathroom when the nurse will need to stay overnight, but there is also a TV room for privacy. In Nashville, there were three TVs, but here there is only one which I haven't turned on. Not much need for distraction when you are in paradise.

Sunday is a quiet day. We seem to be pacing ourselves in this newfound semi-relationship. I make a point not to try to cover everything I would like to say to her. There will be time, I hope. In case there isn't, I have been recording stories of my life to leave her.

We drive down to the Mauna Kea Beach. I sit while Michelle walks Rhett on his leash. I'm glad we brought the beach umbrella. I like the shade more these days. There was a time when I would lie in the sun and have the energy to chase after girls. What little energy awarded me is reserved for sitting in the shade and watching the girls walk by. I take out a small notebook and write:

THE GOOD OLD DAYS
There was a time
in my natural prime
when the young girls thought I was fine
now I just sit in the shade
remembering when I had it made
or thought I did
if you can remember the good old days
then these are the good old days.

Michelle, and a panting Rhett, plop down beside me. Rhett drinks out of his blue plastic water bowl so loudly the other beach patrons must think there was a tsunami roaring ashore.

"Max, where are you going to be buried?"

I'm taken aback by her abrupt question. Then I realized our minds are alike—she had wandering thoughts while walking Rhett. "I was hoping for a Viking funeral."

"A Viking funeral?"

"Sure. Ever see a Viking movie where they place the body of their King in a wooden boat stacked with firewood and set him adrift out to sea and then the archers shoot flaming arrows onto the boat from the shore and the dude goes out in a blaze of fire and glory as the sun is setting? That is how I want to go. Max Largent *aka* Thor, no more."

"No, seriously."

I laugh even if she doesn't. "I have left instructions with the Hospice Center to be cremated and to hire someone to paddle out at sunset and sprinkle my ashes here on the waters off Mauna Kea Beach. As you can see, it is one of the most beautiful places on God's planet."

"Have you ever brought any of your girlfriends here?"

"No woman other than you."

She likes that, maybe because I referred to her as a woman or the exclusivity we are sharing. Based on my sorted history with women, I would say it's the exclusivity. They seem to like that as in, *Am I the prettiest girl you ever dated?* and if you answer that with anything other than a resounding *"YES!"* you deserve to be shot.

It is true she is the only woman I have been with at Mauna Kea and I actually hadn't thought of it before but I am glad it is with her.

5 1

THE ARTIST

My head is pounding like a *pa'u* drum, but I don't want Michelle to know. I'm so enjoying our time together. Sending up gratitude again—as I do several times each day—that this sweet girl has been here. It feels like she has been here one day but it's more like six or is it eight?

Michelle asks, "Do you want a cup of tea or anything before the art teacher arrives?"

I forgot this is watercolor painting day. Sighing, I reply, "Aw, Michelle. I'd like to go take a nap instead. I should have canceled our appointment with Beth, but I forgot. When she arrives, please pay her and tell her I'm sorry but don't feel up to it."

"Of course," she says but her look of concern twists my heart.

In my head, I mosey off to my bed, but in reality, I'm shuffling like a man who can't feel his feet. If I lie just right I can watch Michelle in the living room paint on her easel.

I'm situated and comfortable as possible given my condition with Rhett by my side before the doorbell rings. I hear Beth White before I see her. She is a true island art teacher. She exudes warmth with an engaging smile of perfectly white teeth that highlight a tanned and lined round face with long white hair that cascades over brown shoulders. She usually wears a full flowing cotton dress decorated with prints of colorful flowers, and I imagine today is no different. Her intelligent bright brown eyes declare that they were painted by the earth. This lady is a walking, talking advertisement for serene island living.

I hear Michelle explain that, "Hi, I am Michelle, Max is not feeling well and since he didn't cancel the session, he wants to pay for today. Please come in for a visit." No explanation of who she is, other than her name, or our relationship.

I hear Beth's upbeat voice reply, "I would love to."

Michelle brings Beth into the dining area and I can glimpse her staring at the easel. Michelle has started a penciled outline for a new painting. "What is this going to be?" Beth asks.

"I'm not sure yet. Maybe *Man on a Beach*," Michelle says pointing to my painting. "I finished Max's watercolor of a yellow and white orchid that you've been helping him with."

I can hear the smile in Beth's voice as she says, "That's wonderful. Now it has both of your energies. I can also tell which one of you is the artist and which one was my student." Then she laughs.

I smile. Now I know why I like this woman.

Michelle offers her tea, and they settle at the other end of the dining room table. I'm glad because it brings me joy, and distracts from the pain in my head, to eavesdrop on their visit. Plus, Michelle is nearby if I need her—which I hope I won't.

Beth and Michelle talk about art and the different mediums. Beth pulls out her portfolio and shows Michelle some of her work.

"Wow!" Michelle exclaims. "I can't believe you are self-taught."

I hear her tell Michelle how she teaches at hotels and for visiting children but also has some adult clients and some of her clients are tourists who come back every year. "I sell my watercolors and prints at two galleries on the Big Island and the farmer's market in Waimea."

"How long have you been here?" Michelle asks.

"I've lived on the Island for 15 years and will never leave. This is my spiritual home."

"Does everyone on this Island feel that way?" Michelle asks before sharing her own background as an art major in college with a teacher's certificate.

Beth says, "The Island is always looking for teachers. It is expensive to live here, and the pay is not great, but what teacher's pay is?"

Michelle takes a sip of her tea. "I love it here, but I am a born-and-bred Houston girl, so I have mall issues."

Beth laughs, "Honolulu has two malls and they need art teachers too."

They finish their tea and Beth says, "You should come to my art booth and hang out with me. I'm at the upper farmer's market in Waimea on Saturdays. Bring Rhett."

"I'll look forward to it," Michelle says.

Rhett shifts from my side and joins Michelle and Beth as they walk to the front door. Michelle will see Beth's bright yellow Mini Cooper convertible with the license plate that reads "Tweetie."

An artist who is loving and living the creative life in Hawaii.

5 2

DANCING IN THE RAIN

It's been several days since Beth, the art teacher, was here. Although I am feeling weaker every day I would like to go with Michelle and Rhett to Mauna Kea beach one more time.

Off we go on this late afternoon, with Michell driving. I take in every aspect, notching sites and buildings that have previously been driven by in a blur. It's like I am memorizing every detail in case I need to draw a map from memory.

We make our way from the parking lot with Michelle carrying the beach chairs.

I have on a windbreaker jacket, a white, long sleeve shirt and tan khaki pants to guard against my cold nature these days. After resting in the chairs for a few minutes where I continued the vigilant mental recording of all sights, scents, and sounds.

It is time. "Let's walk to the water's edge, Rhett will stay here."

With sun hats on and covered in enough 30 SPF to block the sun all the way to Honolulu, we walk at my limited pace across the warm cushy sand. There are no rocks or pebbles on the Mauna Kea beach. We reach the wet sand and the cool lapping ocean water covers our feet and ankles, I am chilled by the slight wind. This time of day the waves that find their way to the shore are gentle. I look back and Rhett is standing guard by our chairs but not taking his eyes off us.

Michelle says, "You're quiet. You seem at peace."

"I call it dancing in the rain."

"What's that?"

"That, my dear, is the new much improved Max Largent theory of surviving and thriving."

"New?"

"New to me. It took my days being numbered to realize my days are numbered. It is human nature to believe we are going to live a long time, and the younger you are, the longer you feel you have, which of course is not true. I am going out a winner by living my last days, every day, in awareness of as many moments as I can. Being cognizant that every day is not going to have bliss. When those moments arrive, if I can do something about it I will, and if I can't then I'll dance."

"Dance?"

"Yep, dance like I am all by myself with no one to impress."

"Where did you get that?"

"As a kid, when it was raining without lightning Grandmother Jean would let me play in the rain. When the rain came tumbling down, I would put on shorts, no shirt, and run outside barefoot leaping and sliding in the mud with joy. I'd laugh and with my arms stretched and head tilted back, I'd stick my tongue out and catch the raindrops. I was as free as one could ever be. I was dancing in the rain while others were ducking their soaked heads and sprinting for cover.

"In life, it is going to rain on you, and when it does you have two options—run for cover or just let go and dance in the rain."

I shrug. "The only thing we have any semblance of control

over in this life is our attitude. As the Buddhists say, 'Find joy in the sorrow.'"

"What is the joy in your sorrow, today?" she asks.

"I've found you." I look down at the gentle bubbles of the water lapping at our feet. "Let me share with you my observations of this moment."

She nods in agreement.

"I have moments of negativity, but they go away quickly when I remind myself to just be. Standing here I notice my breathing and observe the quiet sensations of this slice of paradise, such as standing here in cool water that feels like velvet on my legs as the small waves ebb and flow. I am aware of the sand gently giving way between my toes and welcoming the sun. Listening to the lapping waves, and in the distance children's squeals mixed with laughter, I turn around and take in the mountains behind us. The easy part is basking in that radiant smile of yours. In this moment I don't have cancer, I have life, and I am dancing in the rain. As someone smarter than me said, 'You don't only live once. You only die once; you live every day.'"

With raised arms, the palms of my hands skyward, I slowly make a 360 degrees turn. In slow motion, taking in every aspect of this world, this life, I look at Michelle and I place my rough hand on her soft cheek and say, "Thank you."

She doesn't reply, only looks straight into my eyes like we are meeting for the first time. She smiles that smile that lights up my world.

A thought comes up that I have to share.

"Michelle, the only thing more magical than making a memory is being aware you are."

She smiles a blissful knowing smile

We are connected.

THAT EVENING MICHELLE and I are in the living room where I am laying on the couch supported by bed pillows. We are comfortable in our silence. It is serene and carries over from the joy on the beach. Michelle breaks the silence. "Max, do you think it is okay if I keep Rhett?"

With heart pounding, my soul sings. For a long moment I can't speak but feel my face warming. I can't help it. My eyes pool and tears slide down my face "Don't make me come over there and love you. This takes away my only worry, thank you." Rhett understands as he leaves my side and goes to Michelle.

A COUGH BEGINS; it won't go away. At first, it's an occasional tickle in the back of my throat but it becomes persistent. My chest hurts. It was difficult to sleep that night and the next day the cough is worse. Time for at-home nursing care.

I reluctantly allow them to call the doctor. Dr. Faye Drysdale is a petite pretty woman with perfectly coiffed blonde hair with a caring but serious demeanor. She has a pleasant bedside manner. She tells us, "I found my way to Hawaii *via* Kentucky."

Her slight Southern accent reminds me of home.

After listening to my chest, Dr. Drysdale states, "Max, it seems you have pneumonia."

Slipping off the oxygen mask. "Leave it to me to get pneumonia in Hawaii."

She smiles.

Michelle looks so worried I regret allowing her to move in. But only for a second. I've treasured every moment we have shared.

They don't realize I can hear them as the doctor informs her, "Prepare yourself. His immune system is so weak. Likely too weak to fight this."

THE NURSES, BETTY and Kalani, are sweet and attentive—to both of us. This makes me happy. Michelle spends most of her time in my room. We sit and talk about life. She reads to me. I've encouraged her to read from *The Essential Works of Rumi* and from Eckhart Tolle's *Practicing the Power of Now*. Is it innate that I want to be a positive influence on her? There are times I can see from her expression that something she's read has an impact. She's really thinking about it, taking it to heart. To lighten things I joke, "Remember, you're supposed to be practicing mindfulness."

She doesn't chuckle. Maybe she didn't hear me. I'm too tired to repeat it.

WHEN MICHELLE RETURNS from taking Rhett for a walk, they both come into the bedroom for a visit. I hand her an envelope. "Give this to Uncle Billy Bob when he gets here."

"Uncle Billy Bob is coming here?" she asks.

I reply, "He will after I am gone."

"Have you talked to him?"

"Nope."

"Why is he coming?"

"Because he is Billy Bob."

After Michelle takes the letter I say, "Here." I hand her my silver bracelet with the thirteen bear paws I've worn every day since the year my daughter was born. "I want you to have this."

She cries, I just realize, I called her daughter.

ONE AFTERNOON I wake to find Michelle reading *People* magazine with a cover story about someone who was famous for being famous. I motion for a pen and paper and am barely able to scribble: "Be Your Own Celebrity." I hand her the slip of paper and close my eyes once I see her reaction. I can't help but smile.

Later—that day, that night, the next day—does it matter? I only care that she is with me. Am I hanging on for more time with her? We talk about spirituality. It's a struggle to breathe and speak, but I must. "It doesn't matter what religion or spiritual practice you follow, as long as it is not extreme—and you live it." I pause to suck in another breath. "Find the one belief that resonates with your soul, you will know it when it finds you."

I doze off but when I open my eyes, she is still there.

She gives me her sunshine smile and I see a glint from her brimming eyes before I doze again.

RHETT NEVER LEAVES my side, except when Michelle takes him for walks.

Nurse Betty tries to take the towel she dries me with after a bath. "No. Stop, please don't wash. I want to leave my scent for Rhett after I'm gone." She nods.

Late nights are the hardest, with fits of coughing. I'm sure they can hear it on the other side of the house. I'm saddened that the nurses and Michelle must be burdened by it.

Once, Michelle came in and said nothing. She curled up on the chair she always sits in and shut her eyes. I was thankful for that. I don't want to see pity in her eyes.

When the coughing fit subsided and I had the oxygen mask on once more, she whispered, "You never complain, Max. Never."

I didn't respond for a bit. Maybe she thought I'd slipped into sleep. When I felt my voice would be steady. "I read that brain tumor patients sometimes get irritable. I don't want to be that way around you."

I CALLED NURSE Kalani to help me to the toilet. How can you feel both humiliated and grateful?

As she shuts the door I say, "Now Kalani, don't go far; I don't want to die like Elvis, the King on his throne."

She has a joyful and full laugh. It makes my soul sing. This eases my bruised pride that she will have to help me off this throne.

Kalani is such a joyful woman, she doesn't realize I hear their conversation from the kitchen.

"That man is amazing," I hear her say.

"Why?" Michelle's voice sounds high-pitched, scared maybe.

Kalani recounts our throne room visit.

Then I hear her pause before she says, "May I ask you something personal?"

"Sure."

"Is he your daddy?"

"Yes he is, we just don't look alike."

"Child, you don't have to look alike for people to know that; just look at how he lights up whenever you come into the room."

That evening Michelle comes in to tell me goodnight. She takes my hand that now seems smaller than it used to be. Her hand is soft in mine and her eyes are warm as she gazes at me. We've known each other for such a short time yet I have a deep connection.

I hear her softly say, "I love you, daddy."

I open my eyes and with a quivering hand take off my oxygen mask. "I know," I whisper. "I love you, too, my daughter."

I close these tired eyes, and she gently wipes away tears that are dripping down my face.

53

MICHELLE

Max Largent died this morning.

It has been nine days since we were at the beach. He died from a heart attack caused by fluid in his lungs. He had said, "I'm not going to let cancer beat me on its terms."

"I think he knew what he was doing standing in that cool water with the wind blowing on him," I told the Doctor. "He was ready to go and he went on his terms."

"He sounds like a determined man," said Dr. Faye Drysdale.

"I was starting to discover that."

Both the doctor and nurse looked quizzically at me but I was too tired to explain my unique relationship with Max.

If there ever was a word to define John Maxwell Largent, it is unique.

WHEN I TALKED about my childhood, he would listen with intense and sometimes watery eyes. I know he enjoyed learning about me, but there had to have been a part of him that missed knowing me as his child.

I have grown up a lot in the past few weeks, faced angers of the past, which now seem so trivial. I found—and lost—my biological father. I still cherish the father who raised me, Ted Miller, but I believe it does not take away from his memory to also call Max "Dad."

Max had asked Ms. Freeman at the rental company if I could stay here until the lease was up and she kindly agreed.

Except for Max's coughing, the house was quiet during those last few days. I painted, read, walked Rhett, did some food shopping and arranged for the rental car company to pick up Max's car. They charged a fee but were nice about it when I said he was too ill to return it.

I called Mom every couple of days. She offered to come over but I knew, as Max would say, that I needed that like Custer needed more Indians. Oh my gosh, I am starting to think like him! Scary!

WHEN MAX DIED this morning, he died knowing he was loved and I believe in my heart he was able to accept being loved, at last.

Kalani woke me at 2:00 AM and told me, "He's slipping away."

I put on my robe and went in to sit beside his bed and held his hand. His other hand rested on Rhett's head.

Max's eyes were the clearest green I had ever seen and his face looked the most peaceful any human could. A gurgling sound came from his throat, his lips parted, and he said a word I couldn't hear through my sobbing.

I quickly asked Kalani, "What did he say?"

She replied with tears in her eyes "Child, his last word was 'Grace.' You brought that to him."

I lost it, I sat there for over an hour sobbing, holding his hand, and petting Rhett who was whimpering in the most mournful sound I have ever heard. I sat there for over an hour just holding his hand. Amazingly, his fingers and palm stayed warm the entire time.

I thought about how little time I have known him and how, in these micro-moments, I have learned so much about him—and about me. And while I didn't understand everything from our conversations, my time here has awakened in me the desire to learn more about life, spirituality, and love.

Thank you, Max.

KALANI CALLES THE EMS and they are here to take him to the crematory. I let go of my father's hand for the last time.

Rhett, Kalani, and I follow them out to the ambulance. I ask the driver, "Would you be kind enough to put on the emergency flashing lights so we can follow him down the highway in the early morning dark?"

The sleepy-eyed driver says, "Sure, but I can't turn on the siren."

"Thank you," is all I can say. I feel like I'm hiding a family secret. Besides, it reminds me of what Uncle Billy Bob said: "You hear a siren; someone has a problem."

Max would like departing, in a blaze of flashing lights.

The three of us huddle in the cool darkness watching the flashing red and blue descend the long drive to the main road, turn left, and slowly—which I think the sleepy driver did for us—disappear into the distance.

It requires a lot of coaxing and pleading to get Rhett to come inside. He just stands in the drive as if Max is going to reappear any minute.

I ask Kalani, "Can you spend the night?" It's too late for her to drive home and I am not ready to be in an empty house.

That night Rhett and I sleep in Max's bed with the doors open and the breeze flowing through.

I am sleeping in Max's essence. I lie here face down with my arms spread out like I am trying to hug him one last time.

I DON'T CRY the next day when I tell Mom, "Max has died." But she does.

"I plan to stay for a few more weeks," I say. "I have a lot of thinking to do." Then I add, "You have that grandson you always wanted. His name is Rhett."

When I call Uncle Billy Bob to tell him Max is gone, I do cry.

He says, "I'm coming. I'll be on the first thing smoking."

"You don't need to, I am okay."

"No, I want to. Besides, I got to settle up with the hospice and take care of some things."

"That is just an excuse."

"I know. But it's the best one I got and it will have to do, young lady."

I keep busy the next two days until Billy Bob arrives by working on watercolor painting and organizing Max's personal things to be given to the hospice to sell. I keep a few things like some of his books, his computer, and a dark blue windbreaker jacket that reminds me of him when we would sit and watch the stars. There are also notes and tapes of the book he wanted published, his poems, and a second set of tapes labeled, *The Laughs and Time of Max Largent*. A note secured to them with a green rubber band states; "Michelle, these will help answer your questions about how I thrived 44 years on this round ball."

Rhett and I take walks—when he isn't lying on Max's bed with the towel. He will come into my room when I go to sleep and lie with me for 20 or so minutes, then he goes and lies by the door, which I think of as his guard dog duty.

The first two days Rhett roamed around the house and yard like he was looking for his lost best friend. On the morning of the second day, the crematory was kind enough to deliver Max's ashes. They inform me that everything was prepaid. I call hospice and tell them I will take care of spreading his ashes, which I plan to do after Uncle Billy Bob leaves. I put the urn in the middle of the dining room table since that is where Max liked to look out late at night when not on the lanai.

Mom calls, which is okay except I have nothing new to say, but I know it makes her feel like she is helping.

I asked Max to "Tell me about his mother" but he just smiled and said. "Everything you need to know is on the tapes and in the book." He did volunteer that, "She was like all of us, not as guilty as she seemed, or as innocent as she liked us to believe."

UNCLE BILLY BOB arrives today.

Rhett and I meet him at the Kona airport and, as always, he is happy-go-lucky, full of energy and, as Max would say, "He could put fun in funeral." Until we get to the house.

When he sees Max's urn, I thought he was going to lose it, but he rallies and talks about the view and what a great house it is, all while he moves around like a nervous cat, afraid to stay in one place because it might remind him of the dark reason he is here. I direct him to the other guest room, where he unpacks.

I hand him a beer which is a Budweiser. "Oh good. An import."

That is true—in Hawaii. We sit on the lanai and talk about his uneventful trip and I get up and retrieve the letter Max left him.

I leave him alone to read it. When I came back Billy Bob's eyes are red and watery.

"I have known that man for 24 years and I will never understand him. A loner's loner who loved people—especially women—yet couldn't or wouldn't trust anyone with his heart except for that bear of a dog. And this is bull crap, wanting to die alone halfway around the world with no funeral or memorial service. Me? I am going to have the biggest funeral in Texas with so many pretty ladies you can sell tickets."

It is easy to tell this bravado is an attempt to hide his sadness. I smile and look at the note lying on the side table beside his lounge chair.

When he notices this, he says, "He wanted to thank me again for taking care of business and Rhett's trust fund. Wanted to let me know he forgave me for not telling him about you and that he understood that I had given my word to your mom. He reminded me he knew how important keeping my word is to me—and that is why I was the only person he would have played poker with over the phone."

I smile because only Max, or Billy Bob, would make a joke in a goodbye note.

Uncle Billy Bob takes a long swig of the Budweiser. "He also thanked me for helping bring you into his life, making it a significant blessing."

All I can do is ask, "Will you please stand up?" That's so I can give him a sincere hug.

WITH RHETT IN the back seat, I drive Uncle Billy Bob up to the hospice center where he arranges for a donation in Max's name and thanks them for the loving care they provided. I drive back using the same route Max took when we went to Hawi. I think Uncle Billy Bob will enjoy the inspiring views.

When we get to the overlook he says, "Wow, I can see why Max loved this place so much and how it brought him such peace. But, where's the mall?"

I laugh. There are many good reasons people choose to live in Hawaii but I think it is much easier when you are born here and have family or you are at the end of your life's journey, and want quiet reflection in nature's beauty.

Don't know how long I will stay in Hawaii or even if it is here or Honolulu, but I know Max would want me to take my time. As he would say, "You can always leave and you can always come back."

I don't take him to the Bamboo Bar and Restaurant. I will save that as my place with Max. We do drive downhill past the Kawaihae Burger and Taco stand to the Seafood Bar and Grill in Kawaihae. Max had pointed it out and told me he intended to take me there. It is on the second floor and is a local's place that lucky tourists sometimes find. Tall windows provide plenty of natural light. We pass a few tables outside. The inside has a nice Hawaiian vibe with open shutters and a long, deep brown wooden bar. Fishing nets holding antique glass floats drape from the ceiling. Polished, dark, and light *koa* wood canoe paddles hang on the wall for an Island motif. The waitresses are *Aloha* Spirit friendly.

I swear, if Uncle Billy Bob wasn't flirting or looking for whom to flirt with, he would be lost. Thank goodness—if goodness has anything to do with it—Billy Bob is charming with that Texas accent and has an innate natural sense to know when to stop the charm campaign, or not start at all.

Taking a page from Max's book, I ask the waitress her name, which is Kathy, and introduce myself and Billy Bob. I ask her, "What do you recommend for me and my uncle?" I didn't want this stranger to confuse me with some little Texas girl who was lured by a free trip to Hawaii with some older dude. Hey, I may want to live here one day.

Kathy recommends any of the fish. "It's all fresh," she says, volunteering that the hamburger beef is "island grown." I choose the shrimp stir fry and he orders the burger. I like the ambiance of this place—and the charming company.

I ASK UNCLE Billy Bob if he wants a tour of the Island.

He says, "No, I've seen enough. What I really came for is to see that you're okay."

"And?" I ask.

"You are much better than I could have imagined, considering all that has been thrown at you in such a short period of time. I am really proud of you."

"Do me a favor?" I ask.

"What's that?"

"When you get back to Houston let Mom know I'm okay."

"Sure, but when are you going back?"

"I don't know. I still have a lot of thinking to do about my life and this seems like the natural place to do it."

"Well, you know the rent on the house is paid for another six weeks and I can wait on asking for the deposit back."

Kathy brings our drinks—tea for me and an imported Bud for Billy Bob. I thank her and Billy Bob just smiles that million-watt smile.

I take a sip then continue. "Max suggested I stay a little longer to get a real feel of the Island."

"So, what did you learn about Max?"

"Not as much as I wanted to and I look forward to learning more from his tapes and writing, but he reminds me of, to paraphrase one of the poet Lord Byron's lovers, 'He was mad, bad and wonderful to know.'"

"I thought it was 'dangerous to know'," says Billy Bob.

"It is. But what I have gathered is that Max was not dangerous except to himself. He would be the first to acknowledge that and brag about it. It's part of his wonderfulness."

Billy Bob says, "True, but Max didn't want anyone to know him."

"Except me," I reply.

"Then you, child, are a miracle worker."

Our food arrives. My shrimp stir fry is excellent and Billy Bob seems to enjoy his local grass-fed burger. We talk about Houston and travel—to keep it light while we enjoy our meal. I ask for the check and insist on paying as a small thank you to Uncle Billy Bob because I want to reinforce my position that he is my uncle.

5 4

MAUNA KEY BEACH

Billy Bob leaves the next day for Houston, his home of oil deals, interstate highways, and humidity.

On the way to the airport, he tells me, "I am so proud of you. And I'm so thankful you and Max got to know each other, even if for such a short time."

When we pull into the long drive past the car rental sign and up the small open-air Kona Airport, I say, "I promise to let you know—and soon as I know—when I will come back to Houston." Quick airport promises are made out of excitement to get started on a journey or excitement that someone is leaving on a journey.

I thank him again for coming such a long way for such a short time and he promises to tell Mom I'm doing well and looking tanned. "I'll tell her not to worry, that you'll be coming home soon. After all, there's no place for you to use your Neiman Marcus or Saks Fifth Avenue credit cards."

Uncle Billy Bob's idea of roughing it is staying at a Holiday Inn without room service. His words.

We have a sweet goodbye, sweet in the sense that no one cries. I drop him off at the outdoor terminal with palm trees swaying goodbye to all. "Be sure to enjoy this mild glorious weather before you are hit by the intensity of Houston."

He takes in a deep breath and looks around one last time. "It is paradise here with visions of the black volcanic rocks, the open blue oceans, and the palm trees. But, I need oil derricks and off-ramps." Then he gives me the gift of his lovely laugh.

Giving Rhett one last pat on the head he says, "I am happy you two have each other." And off he goes. I say a little prayer that he will stay safe and have at least one flight attendant to flirt with.

Urban cowboys! You may not understand them but you have to love them.

I truly love Uncle Billy Bob, but his presence here, while tender and supportive, has pushed me off my rhythm of island life and my desire to answer some very important questions such as, how long do I stay and where do I go? Plus, it is time to lay Max to rest on the waters of the Pacific.

As I drive back on Queen's Highway to the house, Rhett moves to the front seat and hangs his head out the window, inviting the wind to blow his ears back. I think of how Max must have felt, taking this drive from the airport, knowing it may be the last time he is seeing and feeling this view at 50 mph. Maybe Rhett is remembering that now.

WHAT'S THAT HE told me? Oh yeah, his cookie theory. "Treat every moment as the last bite of a cookie. When we realize it's the last bite of our favorite cookie, we automatically slow down, not thinking of anything else, gliding the joy between our lips. Letting it sit there on our tongue, chewing with focus, wanting it to last forever, knowing it has to be swallowed but not just right now; we are aware of this moment."

He went on to say, "It is easy to remember to do this with a delicacy, a view of awe-inspiring nature, or while looking in stillness at someone you dearly love. The secret is to be present and open for other moments, ones you consider mundane like sitting at a red light, standing in line, or washing your hands. The more you are aware of the present, the more bliss knows you. This is how you can receive even more joy from life: being present, thinking only of what you are doing now, and, of course, eating more cookies."

55

I AM READY

I think I am ready.

It is a bit easier to let Max's ashes go knowing that I am going to keep some for me and Rhett. I found a one of a kind, white and blue porcelain cookie jar at a pottery shop in Kona. In this jar, will rest Max's ashes—the ones not cast upon the waters—to be joined in the future by some of mine and Rhett's.

I am going to paint our names on the bottom of our unique urn. Max would call that true paradise—the three of us in a cookie jar.

KALANI HAS CALLED to check on me. How sweet she is. I ask her advice about how best to spread Max's ashes on the waters at Mauna Kea Beach. She shares the names and phone numbers of her two nephews, Trey and Scott, who are native Hawaiians that have an outrigger canoe. She says. "I can hire them to spread the ashes." Can't get more Hawaiian than Trey and Scott.

I phone Trey, who is the oldest and soft-spoken. He is polite. "My aunt gave me a heads-up about you and your need for a proper ceremony."

Then he explains with a chuckle and fair imitation of Kalani, "She warned us, 'If you boys are not nice, I'm going to tell your Tutu,'—that's Hawaiian for grandmother."

Tutu must be tougher than a green coconut.

Earlier, Kalani informed me, that "Hawaiians don't wear black at funerals; they wear bright colors." She also told me to get a beautiful Lei to give to the boys to lay over the ashes to say goodbye.

I tell Trey, "I won't be in the outrigger. I need to stay on the beach with Rhett." It would be difficult for Rhett to watch me leave.

We schedule to meet at dusk in two days at the Maui Kea beach. Their outrigger canoe is based at the Kawaihae Canoe Club, not many paddle strokes from Mauna Kea Beach.

Max told me one early evening as we were spread out on the lanai lounge chairs, that dusk was his favorite time of day, so I want to honor him by scattering his ashes at dusk.

He said, "You know, Michelle, there are several religions that worship the Son of God, and a few Kings and Rulers have claimed they were the Son of God. Meaning no disrespect because who am I to say anyone is right or wrong? But I love to bask in the Sun of God. Not that I worship the sun, but I worship the creator of such magnificence. Besides, every day there is a resurrection."

He added, "If we have The Sun of God, then the Moon should be the Daughter of God. He liked to cover all the bases.

I order two leis from Nicco Flower Design in Waimea to be picked up the afternoon of the burial.

The lady at the store asks, "What color?"

I reply, "One all white, and one purple and white."

"You must want orchids."

"That's the only local flower I know."

She smiles. "It is done."

"Thank you," I say. "See you soon."

Rhett and I spend one last sunset on the lanai with Max.

Before dusk the next day, I pick up the leis. They are breathtakingly beautiful, made with orchids, vines, and fronds. I'm glad they don't take all my breath away because they smell heavenly. They have the largest purple and white orchids I have ever seen. I put them on and they caress my shoulders. The all-white one makes me feel like an ethereal Hawaiian Princess. I wear both leis as I drive down the hill to Mauna Kea where Max and I traveled on our first full day together. Time travels way too fast.

Rhett hangs out in the back seat and Max is in his Urn on the front seat, riding shotgun. When we arrive at the beach, Scott and Trey are waiting with their outrigger. The two large, handsome brown-skinned young men have coal-black hair and warm smiles that could melt a polar ice cap.

They don't have difficulty recognizing me. There's not another woman on the beach that time of day with a German Shepherd, wearing a long white summer dress, two glorious leis and carrying an urn.

They introduce themselves with firm handshakes and Scott says, "We're happy to be of service. Our aunt has spoken so fondly of you and Max."

Trey hands me a piece of paper, which contains an ancient Hawaiian funeral prayer they will chant as they spread the ashes on the water. They tell me, they will place the leis on Max's ashes and at that moment Scott will blow three short blasts on a conch shell as a tribute to Max. After that, they will paddle off to leave me with my thoughts on the beach.

I thank them again for their kindness and say, "I'm sure your Tutu is very proud of you."

Embarrassed, I realize I didn't bring money to pay them. "May I leave a check with Kalani for your services?"

They smile and reply, "That will be fine." Then they bow their heads, saying in unison, "We thank you for this honor."

Trey takes Max's urn, cradling it in his arms like it's a newborn baby. Scott accepts the colorful leis and they head to the canoe while I read the funeral chant.

Grief for our home without our friend!
The road that leads to the mountain
Gainless Search
I am seeking a gift for you, alas!
Boundless love, Max Largent, between us, alas.

If that isn't enough to bring tears to my eyes, hearing Rhett's whining his goodbye to Max as the brothers in unison gently paddle away towards the sunset, does it.

I realize I am near the same spot where Max shared with me his Dancing in the Rain philosophy. I wonder aloud, "Max, how can I possibly find the joy in this sorrow? I have known you for such a short period of time; I needed more."

The brothers paddle toward the sunset, dipping their elongated Koa wood paddles into the gentle waves in a synchronized rhythm that those raised on the water find natural. As they glide their outrigger toward the sunset I murmur, "Except for the canoe being on fire, Max, you are having your Viking funeral.

The fading yellow sun with jagged orange and pink streaks is surrounded by a slate blue sky. It touches the edge of this beautiful bay, then the outrigger stops. Trey, with dexterity of a native-born Hawaiian stands and spreads Max's remains on the waters while chanting. I can barely hear his heartfelt chant in his native tongue.

He places the two leis over the floating ashes as Scott creates the soulful sounds from the conch shell. The white and purple leis bob on the ocean like they are waving goodbye while the mighty sun and the handsome brothers in their native canoe fade from sight. I cry and Rhett whimpers.

A miraculous scene overtakes me. Without the warning of thunder, the low clouds above the beach open into a soft rain. Intuitively I raise my arms out wide, hold my head back as far as my neck will allow, my face to Heaven. With tears and rain washing my sad yet joyous face, I twirl and twirl and twirl. By my side, Rhett jumps up and down excitedly and barks wildly.

I twirl and cry and laugh. "I am dancing, Daddy! I am dancing in the rain!"

THE END

ACKNOWLEDGMENTS

LA Writers Group for the first draft support, Resa Alboher, and Lisa Worble for editing. Domini Dragoone for the cover design and page formatting. Mohamad Al-Hakim for proofreading and editorial comments.

John Seigenthaler, Sr. for his words of encouragement on being a writer many years ago. To Mary Lynn Ziemer for helping to spark the idea for this book.

To the gifted Artist, Paul Harmon, for his found-object sculpture that is a daily reminder to "Press on"

To the people of the Big Island Hawaii, for your spiritual gift of sharing paradise.

Special thanks to "The Man, the Myth, the Legend" Billy Bob Harris for his generosity in allowing me to share some of his wisdom and some of our stories.

ABOUT THE AUTHOR

Michael has written a weekly column for a Gannet newspaper. He has appeared on *The Oprah Winfrey Show*. He has danced with a First Lady at The White House and suggested "As you are an accomplished dancer and the First Lady, why don't you lead?"

Michael is blessed to live in a small coastal town in Florida where the elderly come every year to visit their parents.

Made in United States
Orlando, FL
19 April 2022